1179

It was in Asia that Bolan first found his mission

As the leader of a deadly penetration team in Nam, he ranged at will across the DMZ, blazing at Savage Man.

One man alone could only do so much in that war, but Mack Bolan did it harder and larger. He supremely left his mark upon the enemy and the land.

In the process he earned a label that stuck. Sergeant Bolan became The Executioner, a legend from the Mekong Delta to Hanoi.

Then another side of the legend began to be heard. Stories circulated among the villagers of a warrior of compassion—and The Executioner became known as Sergeant Mercy.

It requires a special man to carry two names well. Bolan has never flinched from that task. He has never deviated from his course.

Against the Cong or mafiosi or Tiger, his crusade has stayed the same.

Mercy always.

And *war everlasting now*!

MACK BOLAN
The Executioner

\# 39 The New War
\# 40 Double Crossfire
\# 41 The Violent Streets
\# 42 The Iranian Hit
\# 43 Return to Vietnam
\# 44 Terrorist Summit
\# 45 Paramilitary Plot
\# 46 Bloodsport
\# 47 Renegade Agent
\# 48 The Libya Connection
\# 49 Doomsday Disciples
\# 50 Brothers in Blood
\# 51 Vulture's Vengeance
\# 52 Tuscany Terror
\# 53 Invisible Assassins
\# 54 Mountain Rampage
\# 55 Paradine's Gauntlet
\# 56 Island Deathtrap
\# 57 Flesh Wounds
\# 58 Ambush on Blood River
\# 59 Crude Kill
\# 60 Sold for Slaughter
Stony Man Doctrine

DON PENDLETON's EXECUTIONER
MACK BOLAN
Tiger War

A GOLD EAGLE BOOK FROM
W🌐RLDWIDE

TORONTO • NEW YORK • LONDON • PARIS
AMSTERDAM • STOCKHOLM • HAMBURG
ATHENS • MILAN • TOKYO • SYDNEY

First edition January 1984

ISBN 0-373-61061-0

Special thanks and acknowledgment to Tom Jagninski
for his contributions to this work.

Printed in Canada

"Unbounded courage and compassion joined,
Tempering each other in the victor's mind,
Alternately proclaim him good and great,
And make the hero and the man complete."

—*Joseph Addison*

"You've got a weird combination there, Sarge
—tough guts and warm heart. Most cats
don't know how to carry both."

—*Lt. Wilson Brown*
to Mack Bolan

"There is nothing so practical and real as
survival except love. Jungle law, like
love, is no philosophy—*it is reality.*"

—*Mack Bolan*

Dedicated to our peacekeepers killed
by the suicide bombers.

In the words of the President, "We must
be more determined than ever that thugs
cannot take over a strategic area of the
earth or, for that matter, any other
part of the earth."

1

A trap! The word exploded in Mack Bolan's head. He brought up his weapon and went into a crouch, eyes scanning the terrain. The valley shone peacefully in the moonlight, the rhythmic rasping of cicadas the only sound.

Was his subconscious warning system alerting him to a real danger, or was his mind playing tricks on him?

By the light of the moon he could see all the way to the tree line. The ground was flat, covered in elephant grass dotted with clusters of bamboo.

Bent double, his parachute still slung over his shoulder, Bolan ran for the nearest cluster. He crouched in its shadow and listened, mouth open to hear better.

From the jungle forest came the screech of parakeets. An owl hooted. A bullfrog croaked nearby. The cicadas went on with their concert.

A typical night in Thailand.

Perhaps it was only his imagination, he thought. After all, the ground recognition signal had been the right one.

His mind went back to the circling Antonov. He had stood by the open jump door, wind tearing at his clothes, and watched the light flash in the darkness below.

Long, long, short, the light flashed. The letter *G* in Morse. It was the agreed signal. So why this sense of danger?

The valley dimmed as a cloud covered the moon.

Suddenly, on the east side of the valley to his left,

figures emerged from the forest. Almost immediately more men appeared on his right. Then a third group came out on the northern end, straight ahead of him.

For a moment Bolan thought they might be Nark and his Montagnards come to look for him, but they were too silent for that.

A reception committee was a noisy affair, especially when the parachutist landed as far off the drop zone as he had. People would thrash through the bushes shouting instructions to each other, calling the parachutist's name.

But this group was on a manhunt. They moved furtively, communicating by hand signals, and they held their weapons at the ready.

The moon came out from behind the cloud and Bolan could see them better. They were soldiers and wore the distinctive fatigue caps of the Nationalist Chinese.

Tiger troops. It *was* a trap!

Bolan looked around for an avenue of escape. The only one was the way he had come, to the south. Even then it would be touch and go; the moment he left the bamboo they would see him.

He unhooked two Slepoy grenades from his gun belt, took one in each hand, and armed them using the opposite index finger to pull the safety ring. He glanced at the sky. Another cloud was approaching the moon. The gods were on his side.

Bolan waited, a motionless shape in the night.

To the north, a line was being formed, the original group swelled by new arrivals. They began to sweep the valley like game beaters while those on the side made sure their prey did not escape that way.

The valley dimmed, and Bolan sprang to his feet. He lobbed one grenade to his right, the other to his left, then ducked, clutching his weapon.

The Slepoys burst in midair, each giving birth to three

minigrenades that fanned out and hit the ground with blinding flashes, spewing irritating smoke.

The valley boomed, surrounding hills reflecting the explosions, and Bolan raced for the southern tree line, mentally counting the seconds.

The Slepoys—Russian stun grenades—were supposed to give a man six seconds' grace by stunning his enemies, but that was for a given area. Here, the troops had been spread out.

In the end he got four seconds, because on the fifth the lead began to fly. At first their bullets went wide, the soldiers' aims hampered by the noxious smoke, but as they crossed the screen after him, their shooting narrowed.

A flare gun fired in rapid succession, and the valley turned silver. Bolan, a silhouette in the flashing light, zigzagged toward the forest.

A green tracer sang past his ear, another brushed his sleeve, a third ricocheted off his haversack. Bolan felt the hand of death reach out for him.

He ran like a hunted animal, unaware of anything but the tree line ahead, his whole being concentrating on it. Eyes glazed by the rush of air, deaf to the noise around him, he raced toward sanctuary.

The forest drew nearer, slowly at first, then faster and faster, and suddenly he was inside, swallowed by its protective darkness. He darted behind a tree and, gasping for breath, peered back. The valley was lit up like a football stadium for a night game, flares dangling everywhere. As for the players, they were coming at him, their guns spitting flame.

It was time for some counterplay.

Bolan folded out the butt on his AK-74 and changed trees to give himself a better angle. He took a deep breath and started firing.

The effect was instantaneous, for the new Kalashnikov was a formidable weapon, its muzzle brake practically eliminating recoil and climb, giving its handler the ability to keep it on target throughout a burst.

Dying screams tore the air, men toppled and the charge halted.

But they were well-trained troops, and those who had dived to the ground in time immediately returned fire. And now their aim became more accurate, every man knowing where Bolan was.

For all its improvements, the new Kalashnikov had one major defect: its muzzle-flash was three times the normal. The brake did nothing to reduce flame.

To counter this, Bolan began changing trees after each burst. He fired burst after burst, keeping the soldiers pinned, sacrificing ammunition to gain time to catch his breath. On the next leg, lungs—not ammunition—would decide the outcome.

A new group of soldiers appeared in the distance. And these had dogs. Bolan saw them run to outflank him. He fired a last burst and fled.

Now began a grueling marathon.

Going like a blind man, he crashed through the undergrowth, thorns tearing at his clothes, razor-sharp grasses cutting his skin. The forest was pitch-dark, and it took time for his eyes to adjust.

The ground rose and fell, so that one moment he was sliding into gullies, the next struggling up slopes on all fours. Vines kept tripping his feet.

Behind him, he could hear the dogs barking and shouts in Chinese. He had to go faster!

A clear stretch came, followed by more thick jungle, then an area of boulders so big he had to climb over them, another clear stretch, then a forest of bamboo and more gullies. The ground began to slope.

A stream appeared and he hurried up it, hoping to obliterate his scent for a short distance. He splashed himself with handfuls of water scooped up on the run. The heat, the burning cuts, the sting of ants...he felt on fire.

On the other side of the stream was a clear stretch, the ground aglow with bits of phosphorescent bark. He raced through that, then the terrain thickened. Once again he was thrashing through dense undergrowth.

An hour after he began his escape he emerged atop a ridge overlooking the valley, his fighter suit in tatters, his arms and face a mass of bleeding cuts. He ran along a trail until he came to a clearing, turned into it and collapsed to the ground.

Chest heaving, heart pounding, he lay there, rivulets of sweat flowing over his body.

When his panting subsided he removed his haversack and took a drink from his water bottle. He sat down by a tree and strained his ears. Not a sound. Even the birds had retired for the night.

He took another drink, leaned back and closed his eyes, his mind taking stock of his situation.

Eight hours earlier, which now seemed like aeons, he had taken off from an island in the Indian Ocean for the Golden Triangle on a mission to destroy the world's biggest heroin ring, Tiger Enterprises.

Code-named Galloping Horse, a synonym for heroin, the mission was to be the opening salvo in Stony Man's war against hard drugs. Instead of fighting the syndicates at home, Phoenix would take the war to the doorstep of the venal surveyors, the filth, who subverted the health and welfare of good people with the terrible products of their self-interest.

Yet no sooner had he arrived in the Triangle than the tables were turned. He, the hunter, had become the prey.

Where was Nark, he asked himself. In his last message, Bolan's pathfinder had reported everything going according to schedule. He had to find him and fast.

Bolan put away the bottle and untied the head scarf he wore in the manner of native warriors. One side was black, the other a grid map of that area of the Triangle. From his haversack he brought a poncho. He crawled under it, turned on a penlight and studied the map.

With the aid of a tiny compass on the band of his watch, Bolan worked out a route to the Montagnard village that Nark had made his base. If he hurried, he told himself, he might make it by daylight.

He repacked the poncho and put on the haversack. He picked up his gun and went to the trail. As he turned into it he glanced at his watch. A little past midnight. If he wanted to make the village by daylight he would have to run part of the way. Twenty minutes running, twenty minutes walking, he decided.

Bolan took a deep breath and set out on his journey.

2

It was dawn, and the sun streaked the sky with faint rays.

Standing on a ridge and peering through field glasses, Bolan surveyed the village. Judging by the goings-on, it was breakfast time. Smoke rose from the homes, and turbaned Montagnard women were coming out of the doorways with buckets of pig feed. Bolan could hear the squeal of pigs fighting at the troughs.

The village lay in a terra-cotta valley, a couple of hundred huts scattered randomly in Montagnard fashion where the only rule was that no two doorways should face each other in case they attracted each other's spirits. The absence of any symmetry gave the place a decidedly primitive look.

Beyond, in low grassland blanketed by a ground mist, shaggy horses and cattle grazed. A solitary elephant wandered among them, the chain around its leg attached to a boulder. The Montagnards used elephants for logging.

Bolan scanned the village for a sign of Nark. But there was none. Nark could still be sleeping, Bolan thought; nothing new in a CIA agent snoozing.

As the day advanced, people began leaving the village. Some went to the slopes to work fields of rice, corn and tobacco. Women with bamboo water containers on their backs headed for a stream in the hills. A hunter with a musket rode away. A family set out for market, each member carrying a live chicken in a basket under each arm.

Still no sign of Nark.

A group of women, small sacks in hand, left the village and headed in Bolan's direction. He watched them disappear from view as they began climbing his slope, then he heard them pass on the trail, chatting gaily. Bolan picked up his haversack and went to follow them.

The women turned off the trail, took a couple of footpaths and emerged into a field of opium poppies. From their sacks they brought knives and jars, and proceeded to scrape the white ooze that had coagulated on the pods.

It was the second stage of a harvest. The ooze was opium juice that had seeped out overnight, the pods having been slit the previous day.

For a while Bolan watched the women work. They moved gracefully amid the flowers, the colored accessories of their black outfits closely matching the reds, blues, pinks and yellows of the poppies.

Finally he coughed and emerged from his hiding place.

Cries of fear escaped the women's lips as they ran to one another for protection. Bolan could understand their reaction. In his tattered suit and with his bloody cuts he looked the epitome of the long-nosed "white devil."

To assure the women he meant no harm, Bolan stopped at a respectable distance, brought the palms of his hands together in a *wai* and bowed. He knew the ways of these people from his time as a sniper specialist during the Vietnam War, and from his return to Vietnam in search of MIAs at the beginning of the Stony Man operation. He addressed them in the most formal manner in their own language, Meo.

"O sisters of great beauty and worth, a lost traveler seeks assistance. I am searching for a brother, another white man. Does a white man live in your village?"

The women exchanged looks to determine who would

answer the traveler. Finally the eldest replied, "Your brother is no more in the village. He left."

Bolan grunted in disappointment. "Where did he go?"

The women exchanged looks, this time to see if one of them knew. None did. "He left with the Chinese," volunteered a second woman.

Bolan's worst fears materialized.

"If you want to know about your brother, you must speak to the headman," said the first woman. "Your brother lived in his house."

"Is the headman home?" he asked.

The first woman nodded.

"Are there any Chinese in the village?"

"They left," said the second woman. The others nodded in agreement.

"O sister," Bolan said, addressing the first woman, "help me find my brother. Take me to the headman so I can ask him."

She signaled to a younger woman to accompany her, and they set out, Bolan following.

They descended into the village and walked quickly past yapping dogs and bare-bottomed children. Women ran out of doorways to look at him, and someone shouted a greeting, mistaking him for Nark. In the Orient, white men look alike.

They came to the headman's hut, the elder woman coughed—knocking being rude in their culture—and Bolan followed her across the threshold. Inside was a typical Montagnard abode, dark, windowless and smelling of dampness from the earthen floor.

By an open fire, on low stools, two men in baggy black mountain suits sat smoking water pipes. One of the men was a thin individual with tiny, almost reptilian eyes. The woman spoke to him. He came up to Bolan. They exchanged bows and shook hands. The others left, and Bolan and the headman took seats by the fire.

"I am Colonel John Phoenix," Bolan introduced himself. "Did Nark tell you about me?"

"Yes," the headman said. "He told us you were coming." He spoke in English.

"What happened to Nark?" asked Bolan. By coming straight to the point he was ignoring Montagnard etiquette, but time was short and the headman knew Western ways, so it was unlikely he would be offended.

"Bad things," said the headman. "Mr. Nark betrayed by the shaman's son. The son was spy for Tiger."

"When was this?"

"Three nights ago. Tiger soldiers come in middle of night. Take radio and code books, too."

"Where are they holding him?"

"The Tang Mei temple. A Buddhist monastery two ranges away. Tiger use it for radio relay. The temple is on a mountain. A bonze tell us he hear screaming at night. Bad for Mr. Nark."

"Yeah," said Bolan pensively. So Nark got himself betrayed. There had always been a danger of that. Tiger had spies everywhere, from simple villages to government ministries. Half the Bangkok government was in its pocket, which was the main reason the Colonel Phoenix visit had to be kept a secret from the Thais. They would have been the first to tip off Tiger.

Bolan knew he had to warn Stony Man Farm that Tiger was playing back the radio before the Farm gave the show away. On the other hand the show might have been given away already by Nark. But Bolan doubted this. Nark was tough. Either way Bolan had to move damn fast. It was jungle time in the everlasting war once again.

A turbaned woman appeared carrying a tray, the headman's number-one wife judging by the silver on her. Montagnards were polygamous, and the higher the woman's rank in the wifely pecking order, the more silver she was given by her husband.

The woman set down glasses and a bottle of tieu, the mountain people's rice whiskey. While the headman poured their drinks, Bolan took a pack of cigarettes from his haversack and offered him one. At the sight of the brand, the headman's face beamed.

"Marlboro," he exclaimed. "Not smoke that since Laos." He stuck the cigarette behind his ear to save it for later. The cigarette that was stuck upright in the water pipe still had a few puffs left.

They raised glasses, and Bolan downed his drink in one swallow. A warm glow spread inside him, the whiskey chasing away the chills of the night. The headman refilled the glass while Bolan lit his cigarette with a stick from the fire.

Bolan took a deep drag. "How many Tiger soldiers guard the temple?"

"About thirty," replied the headman. The water in his pipe gurgled as he dragged on it.

"Nark said he had signed up three thousand men in the area for the attack on the Tiger camp," said Bolan.

"Yes," said the headman.

"How many signed in this village?"

"Four hundred."

"We could use some of those to attack the temple and free him."

The headman remained silent, eyes on the fire.

Warning bells rang in Bolan's head. Something was up. "Do you agree?" he pressed.

"The men have no arms," said the headman into the fire. "Tiger take all our rifles."

"You have muskets and crossbows," Bolan countered. "Our superior numbers will take care of our inferior weapons."

The headman made no reply. Suddenly the room was very still, the only sound the rustling of a paper skeleton blown by a slight breeze. It hung on a wall next to the ancestral altar, a charm to ward off evil spirits.

"What do you think?" asked Bolan, breaking the silence.

"The men don't want to fight," announced the headman quietly.

So that's what it is, Bolan thought. Nark's capture had given the Meo cold feet. "I don't understand," he began. "You told Nark that everyone in the Golden Triangle wanted to fight the Chinese. You said the Chinese enslaved you, that they made you grow opium and paid you low prices. You said they forced the men to be coolies and took your women. And now you say you don't want to fight."

"Only a fool fights to lose," the headman snapped. He fixed Bolan with his tiny eyes, the pupils glowing like coals. "When I tell Mr. Nark we want to fight, Tiger not know about operation. Now they know, now no surprise. No surprise, no win." The pipe gurgled as he resumed smoking.

"What you say might be right," said Bolan, "but only if Nark told Tiger about the operation. If he didn't, the operation can still be a surprise. First, however, I must speak to Nark. Let's make a deal. If you find me a hundred men to attack the temple, I will pay each a bar of silver. And you, I will pay twenty."

"You brought silver?" the headman asked, his interest perking up.

"I will have it sent to you as soon as I speak to my people on the radio. I don't know how long it will take—a week, maybe two weeks—but you will be paid. I give you my word."

"And if you are killed?"

"That is a chance you take, Major Vang Ky."

The headman started. "You know?"

"That you were a major in the CIA Montagnard army? Yes. They still remember you in the CIA as a valiant ally. That is why I sent Nark to you. I also know about you from your cousin Vang Jay."

"He is in America," said the headman.

"Yes, farming in Wyoming," said Bolan. "We fought together in South Vietnam. I was with the Hmong in Kontum." Hmong was the term the Meo liked to be known by. The term Meo, which everyone used, was Chinese for savages.

The headman stared into the fire, weighing the pros and cons of Bolan's offer. Bolan fell silent; he had nothing to add. What else could he have said? Help me keep America free from drugs? A decade or two ago, the headman's kind had been asked to help America defend the free world in Asia, only to be sold down the river when America tired of the fight. No, Bolan said to himself, he wasn't going to start moralizing, not to this man. Better to keep the deal strictly on a business level.

The headman reached for the bottle and topped Bolan's glass. "I will consult the others," he said. "Please wait. I will return soon." Rubber sandals flapping, he left the hut.

Bolan sipped at his drink. Now there was nothing to do but sit and wait. He pushed the stool to a barrel so he could lean back. Might as well wait in comfort. "Soon" could be five minutes or an hour. He was familiar with Montagnard ways.

Bolan's eyes settled on the jars stacked against the opposite wall. Upas tree poison, he guessed. The Montagnards harvested it to sell in town for pest control. Deadly stuff, a doctor once told him. One touch on a wound and a man was as good as dead.

In the space between the jars, halfway up the wall, was the ancestral altar. It consisted of a ledge over which hung a portrait of a Meo couple in full regalia. Ancestors.

Standing on the ledge was an empty jam jar with incense sticks and food. There was an egg, a bowl of uncooked rice, a bit of sugarcane and a glass of tieu. Offerings.

Next to the ledge the paper skeleton continued its rustling jig. Not only was it supposed to ward off evil spirits, it was a good-luck charm for the house.

Bolan stared at the dancing skeleton. *Bring some luck to me while you're at it,* he told the skeleton.

"Soa! Soa!"

The shout sent Bolan to his feet. He grabbed his gun and haversack and ran out. Dogs were barking, mothers were gathering children and running into houses. On a slope, descending single file, were Tiger troops.

Bolan's mind whirled. Run or hide? He was outnumbered eleven to one.

To run would be to kiss the mission goodbye. He would lose face and the Meo would never fight with him after that, even if he returned during the night. They might feed him and shelter him, and do all the things their sense of hospitality dictated, but they would not follow him in battle. A leader does not run.

But where could he hide? Tiger would search the houses, he was sure. And he knew of no hiding place. Nor was anyone offering to show him one. The women ignored him, busy with their children, the men were at work, and the headman had been gone for over an hour.

The enemy helped solve his problem.

A shout from the slope was followed by a burst of gunfire. He threw himself to the ground as bullets slapped at the houses. A squealing pig ran past him, a jet of blood spurting from its side. Bolan scrambled for cover.

By the time he reached the rear of the headman's hut, he knew what to do. It was the old story: stop thinking and a solution will appear. The slapping bullets had done their job; they had cleared his brain.

Bolan whipped a gas mask out of a pocket of his haversack, slipped it over his head so he could use it quickly, and took off. Geysers of dirt accompanied him as he weaved in and out between the houses, heading for the grazing fields.

The Tiger soldiers went after him. There was a pause in the shooting as they reached flat ground and ran into the village, the huts blocking their view of him. Bolan used the pause to put on the haversack and sling the gun over his chest to free his hands.

The village ended, and he ran into the fields. It was a section that had not been grazed for a while, and the grass was knee-high. He plowed through it, hands going for the remaining two Slepoys on his gun belt. He armed them and continued running, making for the bordering jungle.

A gun fired and a bullet sang past, telling Bolan the troops were emerging from the village. He tossed the grenades over his shoulder. The valley boomed, and Bolan went on running, glancing behind him. A barrier of smoke rose between him and the enemy.

Suddenly Bolan did an about-face and raced for the smoke screen, taking off his gun and putting on the mask. The wind was blowing the smoke from right to left, so he ran to the right to be near the head of the screen.

With his mask in place, he ran a foot or two into the smoke and crouched facing downwind, ears straining over the hiss of the smoking Slepoys, concentrating on the shouting of his pursuers. He needed to know if they would run through the screen or around it.

The shouting drew nearer. They were going to go through the screen. Bolan brought up his weapon. Coughing figures ran out of the smoke. Bolan fired. One burst, two, three. He saw his bullets tear into their sides and backs.

Five men crumpled while three hit the dirt and returned fire. Bolan ducked and retreated into the smoke screen, leaving the trio for later, ears seeking out the remaining men. They were more dangerous because he did not know where they were.

A moment later he heard them, running in his direction, obviously intending to go around the screen now that they had heard shooting, not wanting to stumble blindly into a firefight. Bolan moved to that side of the smoke screen. As they passed, he cut them down.

Eight down, three to go. Bolan moved back to the other side. The trio had disappeared. Were they gone or lying in the grass waiting for him? Or perhaps moving around the smoke screen to see what had happened to their comrades?

Walking on his knees in Japanese martial-arts fashion, Bolan moved to the head of the screen. There they were, crawling through the grass.

Bolan waited, motionless.

From the grass a head rose, the sun of Nationalist China glinting on the cap. Then a second head appeared, then the third. They stood up, guns at the ready, then moved slowly to where trampled grass told them there were bodies. All the time, however, they kept their eyes on the billowing smoke where Bolan crouched, invisible.

They reached the bodies, and a cry escaped the lips of one of them. Perhaps the dead soldier was a friend, or perhaps he had never seen a rifle bullet cause such a large wound. Either way, his cry momentarily diverted the attention of his comrades. And Bolan fired.

Bolan emerged from the smoke and took off his mask. He checked his work. Not a wounded man among them, and for a reason. The new Kalashnikov's bullets, too, were pretty formidable, featuring air gaps and lead plugs. As they penetrated the target the bullets tumbled and mushroomed.

Bolan shouldered his weapon and walked back to the village. On the periphery a crowd had assembled. The people watched him in silence, a silence that had a touch of awe. Eleven to one and victorious. The "long nose" knew his business.

Bolan went up to the headman. "Did you consult your people?" he asked.

"Yes," the other answered.

"And?"

"They agree. A hundred men armed with muskets and crossbows."

Bolan looked out in the direction of the smoke and the bodies. "We will have some M-16s as well."

The headman looked him up and down. "You do not want new clothes?"

Bolan smiled. "You think I will fit into a Montagnard suit?"

"I have Mr. Nark clothes. He big too."

"Okay, I'll try them. Also I would like some hot tea and corn pancakes. And hot water to wash and shave."

"Come," the headman said. "You will have everything you want."

On the way Bolan said, "If it turns out Nark did not tell Tiger about the operation, will your people agree to fight in an attack on the Tiger camp?"

"Who will lead?"

"I will."

"Then," the headman said, "the people agree."

3

The column snaked through the night, climbing the mountain forest. To help them stay together, every man had a firefly in a tiny cage attached to his back. It was an old Montagnard trick revived by Bolan to prevent men from getting lost. Getting lost was easy when going cross-country at night.

Bolan had dispensed with the trail because it was a longer way. He wanted to get to the monastery before midnight, before Tiger put Nark through another torture session.

From his knowledge of interrogation techniques Bolan knew that the best time to work on a man was after midnight, when his psychological defenses were the weakest. Tiger would know that too.

Tock, tock.

A woodpecker's tap traveled down the line. The column halted, the men squatted. Bolan heard some-one make his way down the column. It was the headman.

"We are at edge of forest," he whispered. "Temple ahead. Come."

Bolan and the headman made their way past the line of glowing fireflies flicking on and off. They emerged into grassland and knelt by a large boulder. A couple of hundred yards away stood a compound of buildings with a pagoda. Lights flickered from the shuttered windows, and in the pagoda there was chanting.

"They hold services at this hour?" asked Bolan. It was nearly eleven o'clock.

"These bonzes pray day and night," said the headman. "Tang Mei is temple of Night Buddha."

The entrance to the pagoda was lit by flaming torches. By their light Bolan could see two soldiers. He brought out his field glasses for a better look. One man sat on the steps. His companion leaned against one of the stone dragons flanking the entrance. Both were eating, holding a bowl and chopsticks, their rifles propped nearby.

"Could be they're holding Nark in the pagoda," Bolan said.

"Not know," replied the headman.

Bolan went on inspecting the target. The ground behind the monastery rose sharply to a plateau. On the plateau stood a shack with an antenna.

"Radio relay station," said the headman, seeing him looking up.

"Doesn't seem to be anyone there now," said Bolan. The shack was in darkness. He turned his attention to the compound. "Which building houses the soldiers?"

"Not know."

Great, thought Bolan. Crossbows, muskets, and he didn't have a clue where to start.

He lowered his glasses. "Okay, here's what I propose." He outlined his plan. "Do you agree?"

"I agree," said the headman and went back to the forest.

Bolan put away the field glasses and brought out a camy stick. He proceeded to apply the camouflage to his hands and face. By the time three men with crossbows joined him, the whole of him blended into the night. He gave the men their instructions.

"Wait," said one of the men. He undid the safety pin from Bolan's back and freed the firefly in the cage. He handed Bolan the cage. "Keep for next time."

Bolan pocketed the cage. It was made from a banana leaf. "Ready?" he asked them. "Let's go. May the spirits protect us."

They ran for the cover of the nearest building and crouched in its shadow. They waited to catch their breath, then worked their way along the wall.

When they came to the end of the building, they sprinted across open ground, working their way closer to the pagoda. The next building was in total darkness. They could hear snoring, and a child's voice mumbled in its sleep. It was a boys' dormitory. The monks ran a school for temple pages.

To his right Bolan could hear a lot of loud talk and laughter. Right away that told him something. Thais did not talk loudly, especially not in a monastery. He waited until he could hear the language clearly. It was Chinese, which confirmed what he thought. He took a Meo by the arm.

"Tiger," he whispered, pointing.

The other ran off. He would tell the headman, who would now know where to place his M-16 squad.

Bolan and the other two continued along the wall. They reached the corner and Bolan peered ahead. Before him was a sandy clearing in the middle of which grew the traditional sacred tree. Beyond was the pagoda, the inside lit and visible through the open doorway, though the monks were out of sight.

On the steps, the two soldiers were serving themselves second helpings from a multitiered food container of the kind peasants took to the rice fields. Bolan watched them resume eating. They were completely absorbed in their meal.

Perhaps they were not guarding anything, thought Bolan. Perhaps they were simply having a late dinner and had chosen the spot because of the light. If so, they could not have chosen a better place as far as he was concerned. The chanting would drown out whatever noise Bolan and his men might make.

Bolan signaled the Meo and they crawled out, Bolan following. They crawled single file, trying to keep the bodhi tree between them and the soldiers. Bolan kept his eyes and ears wide open. This was the most dangerous moment; they were completely exposed.

The Meo reached the tree and rose, eyes on Bolan, who lay on his stomach a few yards away so he would have a better line of fire if he have to intervene. Bolan edged sideways to see the soldiers. They were still eating.

Bolan nodded, and the Meo stepped out. Two arrows sang through the air. Rice bowls and chopsticks clattered, one man groaned and fell to the steps, and the other began coughing blood, hands clutching the arrow embedded in his stomach.

The chanting stopped.

The Meo looked at Bolan as if to say, What do we do now? Neither of two young Meo had ever killed a man. One reason they had volunteered was that a Meo was not a man until he had killed. The professionals, the ex-soldiers, had refused to take part in an operation that opposed muskets to assault rifles.

Bolan streaked past the Meo, hand going for his dagger. He bounded up the steps and plunged it into the coughing soldier's heart. The man died instantly, and Bolan dragged both bodies inside the doorway of the pagoda. The Meo followed with the soldiers' rifles.

"Get the food things!" Bolan snapped, livid with anger. He would have the headman's neck for giving him greenhorns. He turned to the line of yellow-robed monks in the interior of the pagoda, gave a perfunctory *wai*, and said, "Venerable monks, sing."

The monks glowered back in antagonistic silence. Not only was this foreigner desecrating a holy place by retaining his footwear, he had the impertinence to bring savages with him.

No love is lost in Thailand between the lowlander and the Montagnard, one civilized to the point of decadence, the other primitive and pagan, but a superior fighter.

"Sing, venerable monks," Bolan repeated.

The shaved heads remained silent. They knelt on the stone floor under a giant statue of the Night Buddha. The god gazed at Bolan through half-open eyes giving the impression he, too, was displeased by this intrusion.

Bolan sympathized, but war is war. He told the Meo to bar the door and went over to the chief monk. He dropped to one knee and addressed him in the most formal manner.

"Venerable teacher, excuse this imposition. I have come to rescue the white man. Please have the other monks sing while we talk. If they do not, the Chinese might suspect and come, and there will be fighting. I have a hundred barbarians outside ready to attack if necessary."

The head bonze and his assistant exchanged glances.

Bolan continued, "If there is fighting, many of your monks could be killed. Many of your temple boys, too. Your monastery will be damaged by fire. Please sing."

There was another exchange of looks. The head monk nodded, the assistant intoned. Wooden sticks clacked, small brass cymbals clashed and the chanting resumed.

"Thank you, venerable teacher," said Bolan. "Where is the white man?"

The monk's gaze fell to the floor.

"He's under the pagoda?"

The monk nodded.

"Where is the entrance?"

The monk said nothing.

"Please, venerable teacher, there is not much time."

"We haven't the key."

"Doesn't matter—I can open locks without a key. Where is the entrance?"

"The entrance is in the rear of the temple. One must go outside."

They held each other's eyes. Was this a trick, Bolan asked himself. There was something of a snake about this man. The eyes were glazed and the voice was syrupy.

Bolan lifted himself to his feet. "Please come to show me the entrance."

A shaved eyebrow rose almost imperceptibly. The monk had not expected that. He glanced at his assistant and rose. Bolan signaled to the Meo to unbolt the door.

"No one is to leave, understand?" Bolan told them. "If anyone tries, shoot."

The two Meo nodded nervously.

They stepped out, Bolan leading. The square was empty. They descended the stone steps, avoiding the slippery blood, and Bolan motioned for the monk to go first. They went around the side of the pagoda.

The sky was still cloudy, obscuring the moon, the monks inside the pagoda were chanting, and the Tiger soldiers in the building were still laughing away. Everything was going like clockwork.

"Maiouk!"

Bolan spun around and ducked as a muzzle flashed. The monk was thrown against the wall by the impact of the bullets.

Bolan returned fire and a man screamed. Bolan fired again, a long, lateral burst. A second voice cried out and something crashed into the bushes.

The compound burst into life. Shutters banged, doors flew open, soldiers ran out. From the hill where the Meo headman was positioned, a whistle blew.

A musket fired dryly. An automatic rifle replied with a burst. A Meo war cry filled the air, followed by a fusillade of musket fire. The chanting continued.

Bolan dropped to the monk's side, then ran to the rear of the pagoda, found the door, and felt for the lock. There was no lock. The door was false.

He sprinted back past the body of the monk, feeling not at all sorry for him now that he knew the guy had tried to trick him. He bounded up the steps and pounded on the door.

"Open up!" he shouted.

The door remained closed.

"Open the door!" Bolan yelled over the gunfire outside and the chanting inside. "It's me—the white man!" He banged on the door with his fist.

There was the sound of a bolt being withdrawn, then the door opened and Bolan strode inside. This time there was no *wai* or kneeling.

"Silence!" he called out.

The chanting stopped.

Raising his voice above the din outside, Bolan said, "The head monk is dead. He tried to deceive me, the door is false. Where is the white man?"

The monks remained silent, eyes straight ahead.

Bolan walked up to the assistant. He placed the muzzle of his gun against the man's bare shoulder, and repeated his question.

"The white man is in a chamber under the pagoda," replied the monk.

"How does one get there?"

The monk rose, walked quickly to the side of the Buddha, and pushed a panel. A section of the wall swung open.

"Get a light and take me down there," Bolan ordered.

The monk took a torch from a wall, and they descended a long flight of steps into a large cave. On a mat, chained to the wall, lay a tall man with a mustache.

"It's me," said Bolan. "John."

"How come they're letting you keep your weapon?" asked Nark, squinting.

"I didn't come as a prisoner," said Bolan. "I came to free you."

"They told me you'd been captured," said Nark. "I knew they'd be on the drop zone. I was in the radio shack when Stony Man Farm radioed your time of arrival. How come your people fell for it? I specifically left out the true check to let you know I was transmitting under duress."

"The operator must have missed it," said Bolan, picking the lock on Nark's chains.

"How can anyone miss a check?"

"Routine, boredom, people get careless. It happens."

"Not in the NSA," said Nark.

"In the NSA too," Bolan assured him. "A few years back—this was before your time—the NSA agent in Tangier left out the true check to tell control he had been captured. Guess what control replied? 'Next time, please remember to include your true check.' "

They heard the sound of feet descending the stone steps, and the headman appeared. "Fight finished," he announced. "Hello, Mr. Nark."

"Hi, Major," said the tall, rail-thin American.

The headman held out a ball-shaped rocket attached to a small launcher. "You know this?" he asked. "Never see before."

"A RAW," Bolan replied. "Like an RPG but makes a bigger hole, and you fire it from a rifle."

"You want?" said the headman.

"Sure, I'll take it," said Bolan. It was of no use to him—the launcher only fitted an M-16—but to refuse a gift would be rude.

"Major," said Nark, "could you send someone to the shack to pick up my radio? Also, the ge-gene." That was what the Montagnards called the hand-pedaled generator used to provide current for the set. When pedaled it made a *ge-ge* sound. "And a flashlight, too."

"I go myself," said the headman.

"While you're there, put a few bullets through the Tiger radio. The big set on the table."

"Yes, sir," said the headman and ran up.

Bolan continued to pick the lock. It was a complicated mechanism. He signaled to the Meo who had replaced the bonze as torch holder to come nearer so he could see better.

"What did you tell Tiger?" Bolan asked Nark.

"I told them what I was supposed to tell them," said Nark, his pale features showing some amusement.

"They bought the cover?"

"They even suggested it. From the start they kept saying, 'You're Russian, aren't you?' Well, it was obvious, wasn't it? Russian weapon, Russian radio, Russian clothes. I must say, John, your tailors are tops. Even the stitching on my buttonholes was Russian. You know, crossed instead of parallel? I saw them check."

"I'll pass on the compliment," said Bolan. After a while he added, "But if they bought the cover, how come you were tortured?"

"In the beginning I refused to talk. I figured if I talked too early, they'd get suspicious." He grinned. "After all, a hardened KGB agent is a tough nut to crack, no?"

The cover for Galloping Horse was that it was a Russian operation. Nark was a pathfinder for a KGB team coming to stir up a rebellion among Montagnards in Burma and Thailand. Objective: to destabilize the two countries in preparation for a pro-Moscow Communist takeover. The Soviet Union wanted Burma and Thailand as satellites to complete its *cordon sanitaire* of China. It already had Vietnam and Laos.

The lock finally snapped open. "There," said Bolan. He removed the chains and helped Nark to his feet. The man swayed, hand going to his head. "What's wrong?" asked Bolan.

"They were very fond of the sock," said Nark, massaging his head. "I never realized such a simple technique could be so painful."

"Yeah," said Bolan. "It can really knock you around."

"I'll be all right," Nark replied, his long legs becoming more steady as he crossed the room.

They went up to the pagoda. The torches flickered in silence; the monks had gone. They crossed the floor and came out. The square milled with black-clad figures, some loading booty on captured Tiger horses. Occasionally a shot rang out as some Montagnard finished off a wounded Tiger soldier. The Montagnards did not take prisoners.

Nark sniffed the air. "Tobacco?"

"They used bundles of tobacco to smoke out the troops," Bolan explained. "With our muskets and crossbows, Tiger could have held us off forever."

Three horses were tied by the bodhi tree, obviously for them. Two had saddles, while one carried Nark's radio and generator. From one of the saddles hung an M-16 with a canvas bandolier containing ammunition magazines, a weapon for Nark.

The headman came up. He glanced from the man with the mustache to the man with the ice-blue eyes. "Tiger know?"

"No, they don't know," said Bolan. "We can still surprise them."

"When come money and arms?" asked the headman.

"In two nights' time," said Bolan.

The headman's tiny eyes held Bolan's. "How you know?"

Bolan glanced at his watch. "In two and a half hours, which is when our next radio transmission is, we will ask for an air drop." He turned to Nark. "Where should that drop be?"

"Valley of the Spirits," replied Nark.

"We will tell our planes," Bolan continued, "to drop arms and money in the Valley of the Spirits the night after tomorrow. This is the earliest they can come. We will ask for the drop to be at midnight. You must send messengers to the villages to tell people that. They must be there to collect the drop."

The headman grunted. "We ride to village now?"

"You do," said Bolan. "Nark and I ride to reconnoiter the Tiger camp. I want to make a final check before we attack. Okay?"

"Okay." The headman turned to the milling figures in the square and blew a whistle. *"Paj, paj,"* he called out.

Watched by bonzes leaning from windows, the Montagnards headed for home. The Tiger War had begun.

Mack Bolan knew this would be a strange one. Drugs were a blatant form of terrorism, he understood that to the depths of his being, and the enemy was as clearly defined as ever. But to Bolan there were even more serious concerns in his recent life that seriously slewed the picture.

Increasingly he was aware of the potential for betrayal. At every turn, politics and nationalism muddied the clarity of the essential task: the clean versus the unclean. More and more he realized the dangers implicit in his hastily organized missions.

So it felt good to be a soldier in fatigues again. A soldier's kind of action was the best way to find out which of a guy's allies were for real. Bolan needed that.

He felt he was edging toward some terrible revelation now. He needed a soldier's faith to see it through. Yeah, this would be a strange one.

4

The trio of horses wound its way through the cold, wet night. First came Nark, then Bolan, then the pack-horse. They moved slowly; rain had turned the trail slippery.

Bolan hissed for Nark to stop.

Nark reined his horse as Bolan drew alongside.

"I think we're being followed," Bolan whispered. "I'm sure I heard hoofbeats."

They sat motionless, listening. The still jungle dripped with water. Far away a barking deer called.

"You're imagining things," scoffed Nark.

"And was I imagining things when I parachuted into the DZ?" said Bolan. He twisted in his saddle and cocked an ear.

The horses tugged at the reins, trying to nibble the ferns bordering the trail. "We'll miss the cast," said Nark.

A gust of wind swayed the treetops, showering them with water. "Okay, let's go," said Bolan, and they resumed their journey.

A little later the trees thinned out, and they came to shacks and wheelbarrows. They dismounted and tied the horses to a wheelbarrow.

"I'll get the keys from the watchman," said Nark.

"What is this place?" asked Bolan.

"A tin mine that went bust," said Nark. "The owners are in Bangkok looking for a buyer." He went off, swallowed by the night.

Bolan waited, rubbing his arms for warmth. This

detour would cost them a good hour, but it could not be helped. They needed shelter to transmit. It was too wet to send in the open air.

An electric generator broke the night's stillness, and lights came on everywhere. Now Bolan could see an entrance to a tunnel and a water tower.

Nark appeared, key ring in hand. "Won't need to pedal the ge-gene tonight," he said with a gesture at the lights.

They opened the mine office and carried in their gear. They lit a stove, cleared a table and started setting up the radio.

The radio was a Shashkov Mark II, a 1953 model, ancient, but the only Russian radio Stony Man Farm could lay its hands on. As with most old sets, it required a very long antenna.

They strung one hundred feet of wire between trees, attached it to the set and grounded it. They connected the Morse key and the earphones. Nark plugged the power lead into an overhead lamp socket, and Bolan switched on the set. The needle rose. Bolan took an earphone and tapped the key.

"Works?" asked Nark.

"Works," said Bolan.

"Toss you for who sends," said Nark, bringing out a fifty-satang coin.

"You send it," Bolan told him. "I'm not as good as the CIA with bugs."

The key was a semiautomatic transversal that was operated by moving it from side to side. A much faster key than the up-and-down one, it required considerable experience.

They pulled up chairs and sat down. Bolan began writing on a message pad. He wrote a sentence per page, handing the page to Nark for encoding. In the message, Bolan gave Stony Man Farm a sit-rep, requested the air drop and gave the coordinates for the drop zone.

As he was encoding the last page Nark said, "Wouldn't it be a good idea to ask for a team of Green Berets? They could help us lead the Meo. That Tiger hardsite won't be a walkover, and you know the Meo—they don't have much taste for protracted warfare. If the first assault fails, they're quite capable of packing up and going home. You and I can't be everywhere."

"There won't be any protracted warfare," Bolan replied. "Washington would never agree to troops. Troops leave bodies, and one of the stipulations on this mission is no sign of U.S. involvement. Why do you think we're playing at being Russians? If the Thais ever found out we staged a covert mission on their territory they'd pull out of SEATO. We can't afford that. You're acting typically CIA. I'm more modest, like the Meo. By the way, how many people know who we really are?"

"Only Vang Ky," said Nark. "All the other headmen have been told it's a Russian job, not that they care who's behind it as long as it gives them a chance to settle a score with the Chinese. They really hate the Chinese."

"Well, they've been fighting them for close to four thousand years," said Bolan.

"Mind you, we're not all that popular either," said Nark. "Some of the things I've heard the Meo say about us made me glad I was a KGB and not a CIA agent."

"That's not surprising either," said Bolan. "Not after Nam. If I were a Meo, I'd be a rabid anti-Yankee. We used them, then dumped them. It was criminal."

"I don't know about that," said Nark pensively. "I don't think we used them any more than they used us. They weren't in that war exactly for altruistic reasons. You know what Vang Jay told me once? Thanks to the Americans, the Meo now have a big enough army to drive the Lao into the Mekong. That was Vang Jay's plan for the postwar period—turn Laos into a Meo kingdom. I think you—"

The horses' neighing sent Bolan crashing through the

door. As he came out, a man in a black Montagnard suit detached himself from under the window and fled down the slope. Bolan took off after him, pursuing him into the trees.

The Montagnard swerved like a rabbit, running this way and that, then he streaked for something white. A horse.

Bolan run full tilt, catching up as the Montagnard was about to mount the horse. He grabbed him by the shoulders, and they crashed to the ground. The horse took off, and Bolan and the Montagnard rolled, thrashing in the undergrowth.

A knife appeared in the Montagnard's hand. Bolan grabbed the man's wrist, his other hand going for the man's throat. The Montagnard twisted and turned, his free hand clawing at Bolan's face. But Bolan held on, and the man's movements weakened. Then he began kicking the way men do when they're being strangled.

"Surrender!" Bolan hissed in Meo.

"I surrender," the man wheezed.

Bolan released his hold on the man's throat. In return he got a punch in the head from the guy's hand, which held a rock. He fell to the ground, blood flowing from his head, but he retained his grip on the man's wrist. A moment later he was back on top again, and this time he did not release the pressure on the man's throat.

The knife fell; the Montagnard was dead.

Bolan found his head scarf, which had come off during the fight, shouldered the corpse, and walked back. So he had been right after all, he reflected. There had been someone following them. Once again his senses had proved right, though this time it was more obvious; he had heard hoofbeats. Bolan still could not explain where his sense of danger on the DZ had come from. Perhaps he never would know, he told himself. Sometimes you just had to trust those age-old survival instincts and not think too much about them.

In the shack the dry, staccato sound of a Morse key filled the room. Nark was transmitting, earphones on his head, eyes concentrating on the columns of figures before him.

Bolan sat down to watch. The way Nark "wiggled the bug," as transmitting on a transversal was called, impressed him. Nark was so relaxed, yet at times the key blurred he moved it so fast.

There was a final, long *trrrrr* as Nark signed off. Immediately he pulled a pad and pencil toward him while his other hand went to press his left earphone so he could hear better.

Bolan guessed there must be a lot of static. He watched Nark write down a message. Bangkok told them to stand by for a reply in ten minutes.

On this mission all messages to Stony Man Farm were being routed via the U.S. embassy in Bangkok. The Shashkov was too weak a radio to transmit beyond Thailand.

Nark peeled off his earphones. "What happened?"

"He's outside."

They went out. "The shaman's son," Nark announced. "The man who gave me away."

"Did he speak English?"

"Fluently. Good job you got him. He would have told Tiger our entire plan." Nark looked at Bolan's head. "We'd better do something about that."

They found an outside tap, and Bolan washed the gash. Then they returned to the shack and Nark dressed the wound with a bandage from the first-aid kit Bolan carried in his haversack.

"We're getting to be quite a team," said Nark. "You pick locks to free me, I treat your wounds." He nodded at the first-aid kit. "You do come prepared, don't you?"

"When you've done as many missions as I have," said Bolan, "you don't forget to bring the essentials."

"The odds are that blood will flow, right?"

"Pretty much," said Bolan. Nark looked at his watch. "Transmission time."

They went to the set and each took an earphone. From across fifteen thousand miles of ether crackling with static, there rose and fell a pattern of *dits* and *dahs* repeated over and over. Stony Man Farm was calling Lotus Seven.

April, thought Bolan. He could tell by the touch. An operator's mode of sending was as individual as a person's handwriting. Bolan tried to imagine her sitting by the transmitter in the radio room, a caring, vastly understanding woman who gave of her very best to Stony Men who were forever meeting other women in their wars.

The call signal ended and the message began. Bolan and Nark both wrote it down. That way if one missed, the other could fill in. With all the static it was easy to miss letters.

The message ended, and Nark sent a signal confirming receipt. Bangkok relayed it to Stony Man Farm, and a few minutes later April sent her love and Stony Man Farm went off the air.

Nark and Bolan decoded. The message informed them there would be an air drop in two nights' time and gave the air recognition signal. Tagged on to the message was a bit of news from Hal Brognola.

A new survey just published by the National Institute on Drug Abuse showed the number of Americans on drugs had passed the twenty-two million mark, of whom three-quarters were under twenty-one. Schools continue to be the centers of distribution of drugs.

Bolan stared at the message, a brooding look in his eyes. "A country's youth condemned to slavery," he said quietly.

THE TIGER GUNSHIP HOVERED like a bird of prey. In front of it was a forest, then a sea of high grass, then more woods. The crew was observing a trio of horses move through the grass in the distance. There were two riders and a packhorse. The riders were not aware of the helicopter. It was behind them, and the distance was too great to hear it.

In the front of the helicopter, the gunner was observing the riders through binoculars. "They are long noses, sir," he reported to the pilot behind him.

"That's them. Prepare to attack."

"Chain gun, sir?"

"No, rockets. I want to test the system. Nap-of-the-earth attack."

The helicopter shuddered as the gunner fired. The rocket streaked for the horses. Wisps of vapor trailed it. It flew over the heads of the riders and exploded in a cloud of white. The horses reared in fright.

"The trees!" shouted Bolan. He dug his heels into the horse's flanks, and they galloped for the nearest cover.

Once inside the woods they turned to look for their attacker. The rocket had come from the direction of a forest behind them, but there was nothing there.

"Could be someone in those trees," suggested Nark.

"No, it was an air attack," said Bolan. He could tell by the angle of elevation. "Hold my horse."

Bolan jumped to the ground and ran to the edge of a clearing. He brought out his field glasses and scanned the sky. It was empty. Nor was there any sound of aircraft.

"There!" Nark shouted.

Bolan zeroed in on a camouflage-painted helicopter rising from behind a stand of trees. A Hughes Apache. It was America's latest attack helicopter, except this one was not American or even Thai. On its tail was painted the sun of Nationalist China.

"Tiger!" Bolan shouted over his shoulder. He inspected the helicopter's armament: a chain gun and four rocket pods, but no missiles. The last was a blessing. With missiles—the Apache was normally armed with Hellfire missiles—they would not have stood a chance.

Nark ran to his side, and Bolan passed him the glasses. "An AH-64," said Bolan. "New kind of gunship. Flies between hills and trees, darts out to fire, then disappears."

They watched the helicopter turn to face them, the crew able to tell where Bolan and Nark were because the horses had left a swath in the grass. It hovered suspended at treetop level, silent, menacing.

Suddenly the helicopter shot sideways. The speed was amazing, a good fifty miles per hour. It flew in an arch from right to left and came to a stop above another group of trees. It hovered for a while, then dropped out of sight.

"Something tells me we're going to serve as target practice," said Bolan. "Let's tie up the horses."

"We're going to stay here?" asked Nark.

"It's our only chance," Bolan told him. "He'd get us long before we ever reached those hills. This way he won't know if we're dead or alive, and he'll come to investigate."

Just then the helicopter popped up. It fired a rocket, then dropped out of sight. Bolan and Nark hit the ground as the rocket swished through the treetops. They nearly lost their horses, which were sent rearing by the explosion. They managed to fight them down and get them tied to trees, spaced apart so one unlucky shot would not kill them all.

From his saddle Bolan took the RAW. "Lend me your rifle," he said to Nark.

"What are you going to do?"

"Not quite sure yet," grunted Bolan. "But as they say in the Boy Scouts, 'Be prepared.'"

They swapped guns, and Bolan attached the launcher with the rocket to the underside of the M-16.

"If I get hit before I can fire this," he said to Nark, "simply pull the safety pin from the launcher and fire a normal round. The gases from the round will activate the launch."

They went to the edge of the woods again, and Bolan knelt in the grass, awaiting the gunship with his puny rocket like David with his sling awaiting Goliath. He was sure the gunship would cease firing rockets and come looking for them. Not that it was short of rockets—in its four dispensers, Bolan knew, were seventy-six of those 2.75-inch folding fin toys—but Bolan also knew that a soldier had to account to a quartermaster. There was a limit to how many rockets the helicopter's crew could expend simply to flush out two men.

And Bolan guessed right. Two rockets later the Apache flew toward them. It came in low and slow, obviously figuring it had nothing to fear from the men below. After all, they were only armed with rifles, and an Apache was built to withstand even a .50-caliber machine gun.

The sky filled with the *whap, whap, whap* of blades. This is how the enemy must have felt in Vietnam, thought Bolan. To an American the sound of chopping blades was always good news in that war—extract, Medevac, fire support, reinforcements—but to the VC and the NVA it meant something completely different. Death riding the sky.

As the gunship approached, the long barrel of the 30mm chain gun protruding from its belly moved, the gunner trying out the controls. Then the muzzle began winking and the sky growled.

Bolan and Nark threw themselves to the ground as a small storm swept the woods. High explosive rounds. Behind them they could hear the horses neighing in fear.

"You'd better go and keep an eye on the horses," Bolan said to Nark.

The other ran back while Bolan crouched behind a yang tree. As the helicopter drew nearer, it changed course slightly. Bolan rose and moved through the trees, adjusting his position to the new trajectory.

A hundred yards from the woods the gunship paused, its gun moving from side to side. The muzzle winked as the gunner sprayed the trees with a long lateral burst. The trees around Bolan thudded from the impact of the exploding rounds. A second burst followed.

The gunship flew nearer. But when it reached the edge of the forest it stopped again as if afraid to proceed, as if some instinct of self-preservation told the pilot a hunter was waiting below. Orders are orders, however, and the helicopter moved over the trees, the wash from its blades flattening the canopy.

Bolan watched from behind a tree as the Apache inched its way overhead, visible through the leaves, the chain gun winking, hosing the woods with its hail of death. The noise was tremendous: the whining engines, the chopping blades, the growling gun, the exploding rounds.

As the machine passed, Bolan ran to place himself under its tail. He cocked the rifle and withdrew the safety pin on the launcher. Eyes tearing from the dust and bits of wood stirred up by the churning air, ears deafened by the constant din, Bolan followed his prey, waiting for an opening.

It came an instant later when the helicopter began turning. Perhaps the gunner had seen something and wanted a better angle of fire. The rotorwash blew some of the treetops apart to create a hole in the canopy. Bolan raised his rifle and fired.

The metal sphere hanging under the M-16's muzzle spun and flew to meet the green gray shape above. It punched a hole in the belly, there was a flash, and a ball of fire enveloped the helicopter. It fell through the treetops amid the sound of breaking tree limbs and shearing metal.

A blast of hot air knocked Bolan off his feet as the helicopter blew up. More explosions followed as the rockets and ammunition went. Bolan lay with his arms over his head while the earth heaved, metal and wood rained down.

Finally there was silence, broken only by the crackle of flames. Around him things were burning—wreckage, trees, leaves, bark, even himself. He jumped to his feet and beat out his smoking clothes.

Bolan heard the sound of running feet. "Are you all right?" shouted Nark.

"So far," said Bolan. He picked up his weapon and stared pensively at the destruction around him. A minute ago the forest was filled with the noise of a sleek killer machine at whose command sat two men. Now that was history, the men vaporized, the machine so much junk.

"We've lost the packhorse and the radio," said Nark. "The other horses are okay."

On the way back to the horses Bolan said, "Tiger must be rich to afford helicopters like that. They come fifteen million dollars apiece."

"There's no shortage of money in that business," Nark replied. "In the States alone, illicit drugs is a ninety-billion-dollar-a-year industry. Ninety *billion!* Can you imagine? Only Exxon is bigger."

"Yeah, well," said Bolan, coming to his horse, "let's see what we can do to change that."

5

From atop a ridge, hidden by bushes, Bolan and Nark surveyed the Tiger hardsite. The place reminded Bolan of one of those company towns that grow up in the middle of nowhere around a source of raw material. At one end was the industrial section with the heroin refinery, a long, three-story brick building with chimneys. Next to it were opium warehouses, a water tower, a power plant, tool sheds, and administration offices. At the other end was a residential section of neat villas with flowers, tree-lined alleys, shops and a park. But it was a militarized company town. The center was a parade ground with a flagpole, and there were barracks, lots of soldiers, an LZ with helicopters, and mortar facing the jungle.

The entrance to the town was a pair of heavy iron gates over which was a flag-bedecked arch. Written on the arch in Chinese characters was the name of Tiger's parent company, 93rd Kuomintang Division.

"They still use the old name," Bolan observed.

"Very proud of it," said Nark.

"Yeah, I guess from their point of view they're a real success story."

"At least someone got something out of the Vietnam War," Nark remarked.

It was the Vietnam War, or more precisely its outcome, that launched the 93rd into the heroin business. Prior to the war the division was basically a military organization dealing in opium on the side as a means of amassing money for the reconquest of the homeland.

This ambition was encouraged by the U.S., which used the 93rd, and other Nationalist army units that escaped when the Communists conquered in 1949, for the forays into China to destabilize the Communist regime.

The Vietnam War changed that. The U.S. defeat, with the emergence of Vietnam as a pro-Moscow satellite, upset the balance of power in the region, and to offset it, Washington was forced to seek a rapprochement with China. In due course the Communist regime was given diplomatic recognition, the trade embargo was lifted, President Nixon toasted Chairman Mao, and the CIA washed its hands of the 93rd. A twenty-year dream died.

To the men of the 93rd this was a bitter blow, and the division began disintegrating. Some of its members turned to banditry, while others prepared to emigrate to Taiwan, now the seat of the Nationalist regime. But a group of young men managed to arrest the disintegration process by offering its members the prospect of another adventure, a much more profitable one this time.

Until that moment the 93rd merely bought the opium from Montagnards for resale to Bangkok merchants. Now it went into the actual production of heroin. Not only that, it expanded into the other facets of the trade: shipping, packaging, distribution—even retailing with the creation of a chain of smoking dens.

Finally it went international, creating subsidiaries on four continents. Tiger's huge money reserves—capital that it had accumulated over twenty years to buy the latest weapons when the big day came—gave the 93rd, now renamed Tiger Enterprises, a considerable edge over the competition. So did its military command structure. By the sixteenth year of operation, Tiger was the world's biggest heroin ring. In a business already noted for success stories, thanks mainly to a combination of liberal laws and public inertia, Tiger managed to outshine them all.

Now it was Bolan's intent to put an end to that success story. But he would do it his own way, fired by personal feelings. The site was surrounded by two wire fences, both electrified, separated by a mine strip. Behind the fences at regular intervals were sandbag emplacements with mortar, and turrets with arc lights and machine guns. And there was only one entrance: the iron gates.

Out of his haversack, Bolan brought a pad and pencil and began sketching the site. First he drew a general map, then proceeded to sketch the individual targets. With the Meo one had to be strictly visual. You could tell a GI his target would be a three-story building with chimneys, but not the Meo. Their language had no term for chimney—in Meo huts the smoke went out through a hole in the roof—and the Meo did not understand the concept of multistory building. Similarly, in marking distance between targets, Bolan marked them as so many hut lengths apart. The Meo did not know meters or yards, but counted length in huts for short distances, while long distances were counted by how many cigarettes one smoked en route.

The sketching over, Bolan designated the targets. There were three primary targets, one in the industrial sector and two in the residential area.

In the industrial sector the primary target was the administration building. Not only did it contain the communications center that Tiger could use to summon help, the basement housed Tiger Enterprises' worldwide files. As soon as the building was secured, a helicopter would come to transport the files to a ship in the Andaman Sea. There they would be sifted, and pertinent information would be passed on to Washington for immediate exploitation. On four continents, agents of the NSA and the Drug Enforcement Administration were standing by to strike against Tiger.

The two primary targets in the residential section were the home of Tiger's president, Colonel Liu Hsiao, and a two-story guest villa that was housing Tiger's fourteen directors while they attended the company's annual meeting. The strike had been planned to coincide with the meeting. All fifteen men were to be executed by Bolan. Personally. It was that kind of war. The enemy would understand no other.

"I think we're going to get some entertainment," said Nark.

On the parade ground soldiers were setting up chairs in a semicircle. Then from a nearby building came a group of men dressed in kendo uniforms. Each man carried a sword.

"The man with the bandanna is Liu," said Nark.

So this is the man who has vowed to turn America into a nation of junkies.... Bolan focused his field glasses on the Tiger president. Bolan always found it interesting to compare a gangster with what he had read about him, and in most cases the real thing was a disappointment, imagination inevitably being more romantic than reality. But not in this case. This man, Bolan decided, was every inch the prince of darkness. Handsome, athletic, he had deliberate movements and a commanding presence.

What Bolan had read about Liu was this: The son of General Liu, commander of the 93rd, now dead, Liu was educated in Japan in honor of his Japanese mother who died in childbirth. The mother was the daughter of a samurai, and in keeping with tradition, Liu was sent to one of those select boarding schools that still taught *bunbu itchi*, or pen-and-sword-in-accord, an ancient art that combined calligraphy with swordsmanship.

He continued his education at a university in England. After being graduated with an engineering degree, Liu served as a soldier, leading parachute missions sponsored by the CIA on reconnaissance and spoiling raids in China. His grudge against the U.S. was said to date from those days. Liu felt the U.S. had sold out the Nationalists and exploited his father with false promises of a return to the mainland.

Liu's dislike of America did not prevent him, however, from taking advantage of a CIA-sponsored grant to the Harvard Business School where he picked up the know-how for his subsequent successes.

At Harvard Liu was remembered for his demonstrations of savate boxing, and for the subject of his master's thesis—the financial prospects of the illicit drug trade, a thesis his professors found amusing in its originality, not realizing Liu was having a laugh at them.

Long before he went to Harvard Liu was already pushing for the transformation of the 93rd from a military to a commercial enterprise, arguing that fighting Communists was a waste of time and the U.S. would recognize the People's Republic of China sooner or later. When subsequent events proved him right he automatically became head of Tiger Enterprises, and it was under his direction that the company had reached its heights.

On the parade ground, meanwhile, the kendo masters had reached the area where the chairs had been set up. They stood around, seemingly waiting. One pulled his sword from his scabbard, and Bolan caught the glint of sun on steel. That surprised him. Normally in a kendo demonstration wood *bokkens* were used. There was also no evidence of the usual head guards, another indispensable item. Even a wood *bokken* could do considerable damage to a man.

"What sort of contest is this?" Bolan wondered aloud.

"The headman said they hold fights until first blood," said Nark.

The waiting fighters turned toward the residential area, and Bolan looked in that direction. Coming out were Tiger's directors, middle-aged men of various races dressed in sober suits, some with hats. *What a respectable-looking lot,* Bolan reflected. They could have been a group of United Nations diplomats. But he knew evil always wore a mask; in fact the bigger the evil, the more respectable the mask.

Bolan recognized one of the directors as Jack Fenster. He was a distinguished-looking man, impeccably dressed, the sort of man people admired. He was a Wall Street financier who lived in Summit, New Jersey, where he had a palatial home, nice wife and children, belonged to the right clubs, pumped iron at the YMCA twice a week and attended church every Sunday.

Fenster was Tiger's laundryman in New York; he invested the profits from the narcotics operation in North America. Operating by remote control, protected by a battery of highly paid lawyers, Fenster was untouchable. Nothing could be proved against him.

The reason Bolan knew of Fenster was that he was the subject of a hush-hush study by the Drug Enforcement Administration that Bolan had read. The study pointed out a dangerous trend in U.S. society. A growing number of rich, supposedly respectable people were becoming involved in the narcotics trade not for the money, but for the life-style it provided.

What organization could offer its members such unusual and varied experiences as group sex in Manhattan with ten-year-olds, boys or girls, a Black Mass in the heart of Rome, gladiatorial combat in central Africa between men and pythons, or pursuing headhunters in remote regions of Brazil? As the author of the study pointed out, for the man who has everything, Tiger offered the ultimate in escape from boredom.

The directors reached the parade ground and took seats. Two kendo masters stepped before them, Liu and a huge Chinese man with a shaved head. They bowed to the spectators, then bowed to each other. They drew swords and the contest began. Holding their weapons with both hands in an extended position, the men circled, feet moving sideways, watching each other across the tips of their blades, *ki* flowing out, each màn waiting for the other's concentration to waver, for his *ki* to flag, so he could move in and fill the void.

"When are they going to start fighting?" said Nark, impatient for action.

"They are fighting," Bolan replied, his eyes glued to the field glasses. "They are fighting with their minds."

"Eee-yiii!"

The attack cry rose from the parade ground, and the bald giant charged, sword raised. Liu watched him come, immobile. Only at the last moment did he move, parrying with a hold-down-a-shadow sweep of the sword. The giant retreated and Liu followed him with a slash across the abdomen. A long tear appeared in the giant's shirt, but the cut must have been bloodless, or he was not admitting to it, because he resumed circling. But now, as he circled, he occasionally retreated, the last encounter having been a defeat for him.

In fact, to Bolan, the outcome of the contest was a foregone conclusion. From the sequence of events it was crystal clear that the giant's charge had not been the action of a man who senses a void in his opponent, but of a man who could not stand the pressure from the other man's *ki*. It was a common and often fatal mistake, trying to make up for a mental defeat with physical action. On the other hand Liu, in the way he disregarded the uplifted sword of his adversary, leaving his head and body open to an impending blow, had shown himself to be a man of courage with a superb sense of timing.

"Eee-yiii!"

For the second time the giant charged, his feet raising dust. This time Liu did not wait for him, but moved to meet him. They clashed, locking blades, then the giant sprang back in what was an obvious prelude to another attack. But Liu never gave him a chance. He sprang after him, and the sword blurred as he struck him with an earth-to-sky cut. The giant fell to the sand, hand clutching his chest. Liu went up and helped him to his feet. Bolan could see the man's hand covered in blood. The two contestants bowed to the spectators, Liu signaled to two soldiers, and they helped the giant off the parade ground.

What a man, thought Bolan. A millionaire, a warrior, and a poet to boot, according to what he had read. But he would have to die all the same. All the talents he might possess did not alter the fact that he was an unclean man who preyed upon the cleanliness and innocence of others. He was true vermin. Bolan put away his field glasses and turned to Nark.

"Okay, let's get the hell out of here."

On the way to the horses Nark said, "I think we should take another route back. Tiger might have discovered the wreckage and be following our trail."

They came to the horses and drank some water from their saddle canteens. They untied the animals and mounted.

"Maiouk!"

From the undergrowth around them rose soldiers, pointing weapons. They were surrounded by at least thirty guns. Following Nark's example, Bolan raised his hands. He would not fight if it endangered an ally.

6

Flanked by their captors, hands tied behind their backs, cords around their necks, Bolan and Nark were trotted past rows of coconut palms. The sun was going down and they had been on the road for over six hours. All of them, prisoners and captors, were tired and covered with dust. Just why they were being taken to this plantation instead of the hardsite was not clear, but Bolan suspected it might have something to do with the annual meeting. White men as prisoners would lead to questions. No doubt Liu preferred his directors not to know of the recent goings-on. That would be bad for company morale.

They rode up to the plantation house, and the commander dismounted. An overly made-up middle-aged woman in a cheongsam came onto the verandah and he talked to her. Equally over-painted but younger women appeared at the windows, and there was a great deal of banter between them and the soldiers, as well as ogling and giggling in Bolan and Nark's honor. White men might have lost the Vietnam War, but they were still number one as far as the bar girls of Southeast Asia were concerned.

The commander saluted the *mama-san*, remounted, and the troop trotted on. They went through the plantation yard and came to a long building that had once been a stable but was now used as living quarters and storage. Through the open doors of the pens Bolan could see rice sacks in some, and beds and clothes in the others. Two were empty, and it was into them that Bolan and Nark were led.

A soldier untied Bolan's hands, another brought a bucket and a ground mat. The door shut and a bar went across it. The troop rode off, leaving a guard pacing outside. Bolan looked around. He was in a rectangular cubicle with an earthen floor and wood walls. The pen was dark and gloomy, the only light coming from a grille in the rear wall. He went to it and tried the metal bars. It was solid. So were the walls and so was the ceiling. He unrolled the mat and sat down, leaning his back against a wall. In this position he took stock of their new situation.

They were in a real bind, he acknowledged. Tomorrow night the planes would come, there would be no one to give the ground recognition signal, and they would fly away without making the drop. A couple of days later an agent would arrive to investigate. When he learned they were prisoners he would try to organize a rescue. But would the headman agree to another mission on credit? Unlikely. The agent would have to ask Stony Man Farm for a money-drop. And more days would go by.

Of course, Lady Luck might intervene, and he and Nark might get the opportunity to escape, but that was a big if. A professional fighter could not base strategy on chance and luck; he had to face reality, which was that Tiger would have a week to work on them.

A week. A wink in time when you were sitting on a beach in the Caribbean, but in a torture chamber it was an eternity. And what if one of them broke? This time Tiger would have the advantage of working on two men at once, playing off information gained from one against the other, demoralizing them with conflicting testimony.

It was too bad they had not had the opportunity to

agree on a common story. The one and only time they tried to talk during the march, they were whipped. Now it was too late. Nark's cell was at the other end of the stable. In order to avoid giving conflicting testimony, one man had to clam up completely and refuse to talk no matter how painful the consequences. And Bolan knew who that man would have to be. Nark might or might not decide on a similar approach; a soldier could choose, but not a commander. Part of being a commander was that you took the rap.

The cubicle darkened as night descended. From outside came the purr of a generator providing the plantation with electricity. Bolan continued sitting, waiting for the footsteps that would announce their coming. They would come for him soon, he knew that. They would not wait for the psychological hour, not when they saw those sketches in his haversack. That would make them want to talk to him right away. And when he refused to answer they would bring out the sock, a sock filled with sand and applied to the side of the head. Nark said that was their favorite tool. Bolan was familiar with the sock. The experience was similar to a dentist's drill striking a nerve, except that the pain was multiplied over the entire nervous system. Still, he would rather have the sock than the water bath or electricity any day.

From outside the grille came the scent of wood smoke. Bolan's mouth watered. Wood meant cooking, and Bolan had not eaten since they set out for the attack on the pagoda. Visions of wonderful dishes floated through his brain, and bit by bit his head lowered, lulled by the rasping of cicadas outside. The rasping turned to music, he was in a ballroom, the buffet table was loaded with dishes. . . .

The sound of the bar being withdrawn brought him to his senses. The door opened and a torch shone. By its light he could see pointing muzzles. The torch and the muzzles advanced. A muzzle rose to his face and pressed into his cheek while hands grabbed his arms and steel went around his wrists followed by clicks. A cord went around his neck, and they led him out into the night. The air was warm, heavy with the scent of frangipani, and the moon was shining. As they passed the back of the plantation house he heard music and laughter. But for Bolan, there was no escaping his fate. Not yet, anyway.

They led him through a banana grove. On the other side was a villa. They went up the stone steps and entered a large room with a stone floor that echoed as they walked. The villa was dark and empty except for a table at the far end, lit by a low-hanging lamp with a large shade. The scene was straight out of a gangster movie, except that instead of a hood or cop at the table there was a tall Oriental man with a gaunt face wearing a mustard-colored camouflage uniform. As his eyes adjusted to the gloom, Bolan noticed several more soldiers on a bench by the wall. He guessed these were the muscle boys.

The interrogator was reading a file while smoking a cigarette that he tapped occasionally against a cut down artillery casing that served as an ashtray. Now that he could see him better, Bolan noticed the man had a dueling scar on his face. But what Bolan noticed most were the man's hands: thin, long, manicured. A surgeon's hands. *Bad news for Mr. Bolan,* he reflected in parody of the Meo headman.

The interrogator closed the file and stubbed out his cigarette. He clasped his hands and leaned on the table. "Do you speak English?" he asked, friendly.

"Yes, I do," Bolan replied slowly.

"Good," said the interrogator as if he were really glad of an opportunity to talk to Bolan. "Now then, in your rucksack we found drawings of our main camp. What purpose would they serve?"

There was a brief silence. "I have nothing to say," Bolan said quietly.

The interrogator feigned surprise. "Is something wrong?" he asked, concern in his voice.

Bolan remained silent.

"Have you been mistreated?"

"No."

"Then why do you refuse to speak to me?" In a slightly hurt tone he added, "Surely the mark of a gentleman is that he is polite even to his enemy."

Great was the temptation to take him up on his offer, to engage in some polite talk and delay the moment of pain. Bolan fought the temptation. "I have nothing to say," he repeated quietly.

The interrogator scrutinized Bolan's face. He seemed genuinely upset by the prospect of causing Bolan pain. If the man had been an actor Bolan would have given him an Oscar. "Do you realize the consequences?" he asked.

"I have nothing to say," Bolan intoned once again.

The interrogator sighed. "Very well." He looked in the direction of the men on the bench and nodded.

A curtain was pulled back, and an arc light went on. Bolan's blood froze. The light lit up a corner of the room with an overhead metal bar and a stool. On the floor lay a pair of wires with metal clamps at their ends. Bolan could imagine to where the other ends led—to a hand-pedaled electric generator similar to the one they had left behind with the busted radio.

Hands roughly grabbed his collar, and he was dragged to the corner.

With practiced movements the men attached a chain to his handcuffs, threw it over the bar, and pulled him up so he hung from the bar, his toes just touching the floor. Only then did he realize that they had just cuffed his ankles as well.

A soldier undid his trousers and pulled them down along with his underpants. Another stuck a bucket up to him and made a gesture that he should urinate. They did not want him to mess up the floor. He did as he was told because there was a man with a raised rubber truncheon ready to encourage him, making it obvious which part of the body he would strike.

The clamps were attached, one to the skin of his testicles, the other to his left earlobe. For the ear a soldier climbed on the stool. Another brought a wet towel that he passed to the man on the stool. The first soldier squeezed some water on the clamp to improve conductivity. Then he jumped off the stool and repeated the process on the genital clamp.

The victim ready, the men disappeared beyond the light, taking the stool with them. Bolan hung from the bar, handcuffs biting into his wrists, the bright light burning the retinas of his eyes. He could see nothing beyond the light; everything was in darkness. The room fell still.

"Now then," the interrogator's voice spoke from the darkness, "permit me to remind you that the pain will accumulate as we proceed. What is more, the pain will last a long time. You would be well advised not to delay answering for too long. What is your name, please?"

There was a deathly hush. Bolan replied, "I have nothing to say."

A chair scraped, there was the sound of a turning dynamo, and Bolan gasped as electricity flowed through his body. The gasp turned to a scream as the soldier hand-pedaled faster and the voltage built up. As he screamed, the whirling stopped.

"I am sorry for causing you pain," the interrogator's voice said, "but you really leave us no choice. I must remind you of what this is doing to your body. The damage could be permanent. What is your name, please?"

"I have nothing to say," Bolan groaned.

The generator whirled. Only this time it went on and

on, the sound of the dynamo mixing with Bolan's repeated screams, the electricity sending his body into spasms, contorting his face. When it stopped, his testicles were on fire and he was gasping for air; the current had prevented him from breathing.

A soldier stepped forward with the stool and the wet towel. He climbed the stool and squeezed more water on Bolan's ear, repeated the process on the other clamp, then disappeared into the darkness. Bolan hung from the bar, panting, his body covered in sweat, the light burning his face, throat parched, tears filling his eyes.

"Once again," said the interrogator's voice. "What is your name, please?"

"I . . . have . . . nothing . . . to . . . say," Bolan groaned.

A warm glow was spreading through his testicles as the body's defense mechanism began anesthetizing. But his torturers were experienced men and knew this. So when the man by the generator pedaled, he did so much faster, boosting the voltage far above what he had given Bolan before. The current seared through Bolan's body, transforming him into a screaming puppet, the twitching body dancing like the paper skeleton by the ancestral altar in the headman's hut, his handcuffs rattling against the metal bar, the pain growing and growing. . . . Suddenly his body went limp.

The generator man stopped pedaling. "Excuse me, Captain, I overdid it."

The interrogator nodded to the soldiers who brought Bolan. "Take him back to the stable. Bring the other."

THE SOLDIERS LAID BOLAN ON A BLANKET, took a corner each, and left the villa. As they carried him, Bolan contemplated his next move. A few more volts and he really would have fainted. It was his ability to withstand pain well past the level that would cause most men to faint that made his act believable.

Bouncing in the sagging blanket, Bolan observed his captors through half-open eyelids. There were four of them, and their state of readiness was zero. They had their rifles slung across their backs, and as they carried the blanket they laughed and joked. Every so often they paused to set him down. The opportunity to bolt was perfect, because by the time they unslung their weapons he would have been swallowed by the night. But there was Nark. On this mission he was not alone. A commander does not abandon his men.

As they emerged from the banana grove the idea came to him. A little ambitious considering the odds, he had to admit, but nevertheless he felt confident he could carry it out. After all, the gods of Southeast Asia were on his side again tonight.

They crossed to the stables, and one of them called to the man guarding Nark to hold open the door to Bolan's pen. They struggled with him through the door, dragged him along the ground, and, sighing with relief, dumped him against the far wall.

In that instant Bolan sprang to his feet and shot for the door. He grabbed the fifth man, threw him inside, took his rifle. As the door closed, plunging the cubicle into darkness, he set on them, wielding the rifle like a club, striking with the fury of a cornered animal, the thought of what would happen if he failed giving him added strength.

Perhaps because the attack was so sudden or because it was dark and they could not see his blows, no one shouted. There were one or two muted screams, but mainly the fight took place amid shuffling feet, moans, grunts, snapping bone, and cracking skulls. When it was over, Bolan rummaged among bodies sticky with blood and removed two rifles and some ammunition belts.

Fighting nausea, for the pen was heavy with the odors of dead men, he examined the rifles to make sure they were not damaged. He checked the bolt mechanism, and satisfied that they were in working order, he left the prison and walked to the other end of the building. The animal pens of the stable had their doors open. All were empty. He unbolted Nark's pen and opened the door. By the light of the moon he saw the American sitting awake on his mat.

"Come on," Bolan whispered to the surprised man.

They made their way to the plantation house, darting from building to building, guns at the ready, keeping to the shadows. At the back of the building, more horses had joined the line tied to the pole bar. They surveyed them from the cover of trees.

A door opened, filling the night with rock music. Through the doorway Bolan could see that the interior was arranged like a bar with tables and a dance floor. It was packed. A soldier and a girl came out. They kissed for a while, then headed for the stables arm in arm. A moment later the door opened again, and another couple stepped out. They too headed for the stables. Would they notice there were no guards?

Again the door opened.

"This is going to be risky," Nark whispered.

It'll be even more risky if we hang around any longer, Bolan thought. The soldiers might overlook the absence of the guards, their minds on other things, but the interrogator would get impatient waiting for his next victim.

Bolan tapped Nark and they left the trees. Bent low, they ran across the open ground and untied the reins of two horses. They were mounting them when the door opened and a soldier appeared. Bolan pointed his M-16 at him like a pistol and fired. The soldier toppled backward, a woman screamed, and pandemonium broke out.

Bolan and Nark galloped off, the horses' hooves drowning out the shouts from the receding villa.

They headed down the road past rows of palms, the

moon lighting their way. As they rounded a corner they saw the gate was closed. The gate was the only way out, the plantation being surrounded by a tall fence.

At their approach, figures materialized. One of them knelt in the roadway, and a muzzle flashed. Bolan let go of his reins, set his rifle on automatic, and stood in the saddle. Nark followed his example. Guns blazing, they bore down on the guards. Bodies toppled, figures scattered, the wrought-iron gate clanged from ricocheting bullets.

"Cover me!" shouted Bolan as the horses slid to a stop before the gate.

While Bolan leaned down to open the gate, Nark wheeled his horse in a circle, firing constantly, keeping the guards pinned on both sides of the gate. Bolan went through and proceeded to fire while Nark came out. Together they fired a final burst and galloped off into the night, free men once more.

For Bolan it was a glorious sensation. He ignored the pain in his crotch although it was aggravated by the furious gallop. What counted was the wind in his face, the moon in the sky. . . and freedom.

Behind them, an air-raid siren began wailing.

Two miles down the road they turned into a trail leading into the hills that would take them home to the Meo village. But here they had to slow down. The ground was uneven, full of rocks, and the thick canopy lowered visibility. A horse could easily break a leg, and they had to maintain a walking pace.

A little later they heard the thunder of hooves on the road they had left. The sound died out at the junction of the trail, telling them Tiger too had turned into it.

"They're going to catch up with us," said Nark.

"We still have a few minutes," Bolan replied.

The enemy would catch up because they were familiar with the trail and would know where they could speed up without risk of injury to their animals. Before they caught up, however, the trail left the thick woodland for a ravine in open grassland. The ravine sloped to a bridge across a stream, then the trail rose sharply up a hill, disappearing into some woods. For Bolan this was their opportunity. He sent his horse into a gallop and Nark followed. They crossed the bridge and scrambled up the slope, reining inside the woods.

"I'll try to delay them," said Bolan. "You go ahead."

"I'll help you," said Nark, dismounting.

"Nark, I'm giving you an order," said Bolan. "One of us has to make the air drop."

Nark was on the verge of replying but changed his mind. Bolan was right; the mission came before friendship. He remounted. "Take care, John," he said and rode away.

Bolan tied his horse to a tree and went to the edge of the woods. Nearby was a large boulder, and he dropped behind it and waited. He did not have to wait long because they were gaining on them faster than he had thought, and for good reason. They had torches, and the woods flickered with light.

On the third horse rode a man with a pistol strapped to his belt. There was one individual who would have benefited from the Vietnam War, thought Bolan. Nam taught officers not to advertise rank by such telltale signs; the VC always fired on officers first.

Bolan counted nine men. As the leading rider reached the bridge, he sighted the officer. A flame stabbed the night, and screeching birds rose from the treetops. The ambush was on.

Bolan picked them off one by one. The ponies in the ravine milled as the riders toppled. The flaming torches that had helped the Tiger soldiers to catch up quickly now helped Bolan to kill them quickly. They lit the target, complicating Tiger's defense. To reach the rifles on their backs, the soldiers had to drop their torches.

But the horses were panicked by the torches flaming on the ground, which made it even more difficult for the soldiers to unsling their rifles.

When the ambush was over eight corpses lay on the trail. Over them stood a few dazed horses. The rest of the animals had gone back the way they had come, along with the sole surviving soldier. From behind the boulder Bolan observed the silent scene, lit by the dying torches on the ground. Not a soul moved.

Bolan shouldered his rifle and walked back to the woods. He mounted his horse and resumed his journey.

7

Bolan and Nark reached the ridge overlooking the village late in the afternoon. One glance at the activity below told them something was up. An armed crowd milled outside the headman's hut, everywhere horses were being loaded with household belongings, and children were rounding up animals.

They dismounted and led the horses down the slope. That way they could descend faster. By the first house they came to, a woman was tying pots and pans to a horse already laden with bales of tobacco.

"What's going on?" Bolan inquired in Meo.

"Chinese are coming to kill Hmong," the woman replied.

"Why?"

"To punish the Hmong for helping white men."

"Who told you this?" Nark asked.

"Ask the headman," the woman said with a nod in the direction of his house.

They rode into the village past doorways from which women emerged, arms full. Piles of furniture and bedding lay everywhere. Pigs were squealing and hens were cackling. The entire village was preparing to move out.

In the square, men were loading a large crate onto the back of the village elephant. The beast knelt with the driver, the mahout, astride its neck. Nearby lay sacks of corn and rice for loading.

As they reached the crowd, the people parted to let them through. Faces watched them in silence, impassive. There was no hostility, but there was no friendliness either. The men were armed with muskets and crossbows. Where were the rifles they had captured? Bolan wondered.

They dismounted and entered the headman's gloomy home. The place was packed with people, the air thick with smoke. A shouting match was in progress at the far end. So absorbed was the audience, Bolan and Nark's entry went unnoticed.

"Did we not tell you?" a man shouted. "We told you not to have anything to do with him. We told you he would bring us trouble."

"You told me, you told me," shouted back a voice which Bolan recognized as Vang Ky's. "You told me many things. But when he offered you money you also accepted."

"Only because you vouched for him. You said he could be trusted. You said we would get the arms and money before we went to war."

"Pao is right," added a third man. "The agreement was for arms and money first. They tricked us."

"Why are you saying this?" Vang Ky retorted. "You know it is not true. It was the arrest of the first man that delayed the money."

"Who are these long noses, anyway?" broke in a fourth man. "I don't believe they are Russians. My son says they speak English to each other. He thinks they are Americans."

"Of course they are Americans," said someone. "They want to destroy Tiger for the poppies. Remember in Xiengkhouang? They were always after us to stop growing opium."

"Is this true, Ky?"

"Is what true?"

"That they are Americans."

A long silence followed. "Ky, we want an answer," the man persisted.

"Yes, they are Americans," the headman admitted.

On the rim of the audience, in the shadows, Bolan and Nark exchanged glances. The cover was blown.

"So, Ky," said a voice rising in anger, "you lied to us. You told us they were Russians when all the time you knew they were Yankees. Tell us, Ky, how much are they paying you to be their agent? How much for lying to your own?"

"Ky always did like licking American asses," observed someone.

"You'd better watch your tongue, Xan," said Vang Ky.

"Headmen, headmen," a new voice called. "We did not meet to exchange insults. We are here to find a way of saving the villages."

"You have a suggestion, Ly?"

"Yes, I do."

"Let's have it."

"What I propose is that we offer the Chinese a deal. As soon as the white men return we arrest them. Then we send a messenger to the Chinese. We offer the white men in return for peace."

Nark glanced at Bolan, alarm in his face. Bolan calmed him with a hand on his arm. Let them get their rancor out.

"And if the white men don't return?" someone asked. "Tiger is looking for them. They have patrols everywhere."

"They might be dead already," another suggested.

"They'll come, don't worry," said the man called Ly. "The one in the black scarf won't let Tiger get him, you can be sure of that. I was here two days ago when he polished off that squad out on the grazing fields."

"Yes, a real fighter," said Vang Ky.

"And lucky," Ly continued. "A man under the protection of spirits. He'll be back, you'll see."

"But we can't hand them over to Tiger," said Vang Ky.

"Why not?"

"We can't. That would be betrayal."

"Betrayal? And what is it they did to us in Vietnam? Was that not betrayal?"

Grunts of approval rose from the crowd. Ly's argument hit a nerve.

"Yes, it was betrayal!" A white man's voice spoke up from the back, loud and clear.

Faces turned and a buzz ran through the hut. An aisle opened and Bolan advanced to the circle of the stools. An empty one materialized from nowhere, and he joined the dozen headmen.

"Yes, it was betrayal," he repeated. "Politics is a dirty business." His eyes swept the assembled company. "As we all know."

At that the tension building up in the room diffused. Bolan could see his message had struck home. True, they had got a rough deal in Vietnam, but politics had its own rules, and none knew this better than the Meo. During their four-thousand-year history they had sold more allies down the river than anyone cared to remember. In politics, no nation is lily-white.

Taking advantage of the new mood, Bolan announced, "The arms and the money will be dropped after midnight tonight in the Valley of the Spirits. The drop has been confirmed." He turned to Vang Ky. "How near are the Chinese?"

"The Chinese will be here in four hours," the headman replied. "They are traveling on the Nam Tha trail. I have horsemen tracking them. We have reports every hour."

"Our homes will have gone up in flames before we see those arms," someone said.

"That is if we ever see them," threw in Pao skeptically.

Bolan looked straight at Pao. "Do I leave the room or do I continue?" he asked.

"Continue, continue," the others urged.

Once more Bolan turned to Vang Ky. "What is the strength of the Chinese column?"

"Two hundred rifles."

"How are they coming, on foot?"

"Yes, on foot."

"Any other armament?"

"Grenades and flamethrowers."

"What about us, what do we have in the way of armament?"

"Crossbows, muskets, and thirteen rifles."

"Thirteen?" Bolan exclaimed. "We captured over forty in the raid on the pagoda!"

Vang Ky sucked on his teeth and looked down at the space between his feet. Seconds ticked by.

"He sold them," volunteered one of the other headmen.

"You what?" Bolan exploded.

"On our way back," Vang Ky began, looking at everything and nothing in particular but making sure he avoided Bolan's stare, "on our way back we met the Yao. They were paying good money." Vang Ky's eyes traveled from the fire to the jars of upas tree poison, to the spot between his feet, and back to the fire. "Since we were going to receive a lot of weapons tonight anyway—"

"Ky thought it was his opportunity to make a killing," another man finished.

A long silence followed. It was broken by the man called Ly. "There you have it, Mr. White Man," he said. "We have thirteen rifles, and they have two hundred. We cannot save our homes by fighting. Our only chance is to negotiate." He added knowingly, "And as you said, politics is a dirty business."

Bolan got his drift, all right. He and Nark were to be the sacrificial lambs with which the Meo would appease Tiger. And judging from the reaction—or lack of reaction—the conference found Ly's proposition a good one. Only Vang Ky had spoken against it.

"What makes you so certain the Chinese will go for your proposal?" Bolan asked Ly. "If I know them, they'll take us and attack the villages anyway."

It was hardly an argument, but that was not the point. The point was to stretch the conversation to give himself time to come up with a solution. He had to find a way of destroying that column. It was the only way of keeping Galloping Horse alive. They could not scrub the mission, not now, not after the work that had gone into it, the effort of hundreds of good people who had been working on it for months, the ships, the planes that were waiting for the signal to swing into action.

He could not let them down.

"The Chinese are shrewd people," the headman Ly said. "They know if they burn the villages, there will be no one to harvest the opium."

To which Bolan replied, "Tiger can afford to lose a few kilos of opium. They'll make it up from their stockpile. But what they cannot afford is to let a rebellion go unpunished."

"There are many ways the strong can punish the weak," Ly said. "A fine, for example. A fine would be much more lucrative."

"I disagree," Bolan replied. "A fine is not a strong enough punishment. The punishment must be strong enough to deter the other Montagnard nations from following your example. The Chinese. . . ."

Eureka! He found it! The solution was staring him in the face, stacked against the opposite wall, jars and jars of it. The upas tree poison!

He would destroy the Tiger column with poison.

Bolan turned to Vang Ky. "Can I borrow your elephant?"

ATOP THE ELEPHANT, Bolan waited for the coming of Tiger. It was night and the moon was shining. The elephant stood hidden by trees a couple of hundred yards from the Nam Tha trail. Everything was ready for the ambush, the entire village having lent a hand. Six thousand bamboo poles had been cut, women had sharpened them into spikes, children had dipped them in upas tree poison, and the men had planted them in the kill zone. Now, the rest was up to Bolan.

He sat in a howdah, an Armalite in his lap, an ammunition belt around his waist. From under the belt protruded a poppy red sash. A black Montagnard pajama suit replaced his tattered fighter suit. To make him look like a real Meo, the headman had given him a broad Montagnard silver collar, which Bolan also wore. The fighter was ready to defend the village.

While waiting, he smoked and the elephant ate. The animal was a nine-ton bull. It stood ten feet high and tore at the trees with its trunk, stuffing huge quantities of twigs and leaves into its mouth.

A birdcall sounded, the mahout announcing himself. The elephant driver came out of the trees, a bucket of rice beer in each hand. He set them in front of the elephant, there were two loud slurps, and the buckets were empty. The mahout put the buckets aside and whispered some words to the elephant. In answer, the beast curled its trunk and raised a foreleg. With the aid of these two steps the mahout climbed on its back and came to the howdah.

"Tiger coming soon," said the mahout. He brought out a cigarette and Bolan lit it for him with the end of his.

"Where is the headman?" asked Bolan.

"Coming," replied the mahout.

They fell silent, listening to the sounds of the elephant eating and to the noises of the forest.

An owl hooted. The mahout replied with a birdcall. At that the headman appeared, barefoot, rifle in hand. Montagnards often took off their footwear so they could move faster, more quietly. The mahout motioned him to come around the back. Big Bottom might get annoyed if he had to interrupt his meal to make steps. This time the mahout had it raise its hind leg. The headman climbed on it and pulled himself the rest of the way by the tail. He joined Bolan by the howdah.

"Tiger be here soon," Vang Ky announced, lighting a cigarette.

"Nark left?" asked Bolan.

"Yes."

Bolan glanced at the sky. "We should have no problems." The moon shone in a cloudless sky, and there was hardly any wind. Perfect weather for an air drop.

The headman smoked pensively. "What if we capture the white men?" he asked.

"You pass them to me and I will kill them," Bolan answered simply.

Just before sundown one of the shadowing riders had reported that a Tiger helicopter had landed near the column depositing three white men. The whites had evidently joined the punitive expedition to distract themselves with a little man hunting. . . .

"Thanks for helping me at the meeting," Bolan said to Vang Ky.

The other shrugged. "An agreement is an agreement. And Ly and Pao are hypocritical crocodiles. They made money from the Vietnam War and now they spit on Americans."

"All the same, I appreciate it," Bolan added.

It was Vang Ky who convinced the other headmen to proceed with the Tiger War. The others were skeptical that Bolan could pull off the ambush. Whoever heard of one man single-handedly destroying two hundred? No matter how clever the plan, no matter how brave and lucky the fighter. Only when Vang Ky announced that his village would go to war regardless, did they relent, fearful of missing out on the booty. There was more than opium in the Tiger hardsite; there was gold, too.

"We should go see," said the headman, glancing at his digital watch.

"I'd like to borrow that," said Bolan. He needed a watch to calculate the column's speed. His own watch had been taken when he and Nark were captured.

They slid down from the elephant and walked to the trail. A shape materialized; one of the men left behind to supervise the collecting of the enemy arms by village women. He led them to a spot where they could observe the column comfortably and from where they could retreat without making noise.

Bolan measured the distance between two trees. By timing how quickly men covered it he would be able to calculate the speed of the column, then he would know how soon they would be in the kill zone. He returned to the hiding spot and crouched.

In moonlit silence they waited for the enemy. No birds were calling, no cicadas rasped, no mosquitos buzzed. It had not rained for two days and the jungle was dry.

A barely audible metallic sound alerted them. A sling buckle hitting the stock. Three Tiger soldiers went by noiselessly, shotguns at the ready. In Nam the pointman always carried a shotgun. For close-range work in the jungle, a shotgun was best.

The main body of the column came. They heard it before they saw it, boots hitting the dry ground, cloth brushing cloth, straps straining. First came two men with M-79s, then some riflemen, then an officer, judging by the map case at his side. Behind the officer came a radioman looking like an insect with the bent aerial at his back. A machine gunner followed, holding his weapon straight up like a priest with a cross at a procession, then a man with a flamethrower, then the commander, binoculars on his chest.

Behind the commander came the three whites. The first two were overweight individuals dressed in golf clothes, M-16s slung over their shoulders. They gave the impression they regretted having embarked on the expedition. Breathing heavily, their faces glistening with sweat, they walked like tired men.

In contrast, the third man seemed to take the march in stride. He wore sensible jungle fatigues and boots, and instead of an automatic rifle, he carried a real hunting gun, a Remington. The first two walked close together, the third man alone, the professional holding himself aloof from amateurs.

The third man was Fenster, the New York drug czar and world game hunter who among his wall trophies could boast two stuffed human heads, one of a Botswana Pygmy, the other of an Amazon Indian. Now he was going to bag himself a Montagnard.

While the column marched, Bolan paid special attention to the interval between the men. Knowing the number of men and the interval between them would give him the length of the column. He had to make sure the entire column was in the kill zone when he attacked. Otherwise the men could escape.

In deciding to attack from the rear, Bolan was taking a gamble. It would have been easier to attack from the front—attack on sight—but from experience Bolan knew that an attack from the rear was more effective. It rattled people.

As THE LAST MAN PASSED, Bolan activated the chronometer and ran back. The attack had to begin exactly three minutes from the time the column had passed. He climbed atop the elephant and signaled the mahout to move out. The elephant lurched forward, the mahout whispering to it, promising piles of coconuts and barrels of beer if it did as it was told. Without the elephant's cooperation the ambush would be a washout.

Soon they reached the trail and turned after the column, Bolan counting the seconds.

"Pssst!" Bolan hissed.

The mahout looked back, and Bolan pumped his arm. The mahout spoke to the elephant, and the beast speeded up its walk, breaking into a lumbering run. Air flowed over Bolan's face, and the sensation sent adrenaline pumping into his system. The charge of the heavy brigade was underway. Two minutes and thirty seconds...two minutes and forty seconds...two minutes and fifty seconds.... Bolan watched the numbers change, hoping his calculations were right because if they were not, Galloping Horse would go down in Meo history as another good reason for not siding with Americans, and Tiger Enterprises' future would be assured for decades to come.

"Pssst!" Bolan pumped his arm faster.

Again the mahout whispered to the elephant. Bolan held his breath. This was the critical moment. The howdah swayed violently, and the elephant went flat out. Bolan grabbed the side of the howdah to steady himself. The charge was on! He pocketed the watch and took up his Armalite. Pressing with his thighs against the side of the howdah to give himself balance, he cocked the weapon and held it ready. They ran through the night, the ground trembling from the thudding feet, Bolan ducking to avoid overhead branches.

"Ayu!" cried the mahout as the column came into view. It was the millenia-old Meo battle cry.

Simultaneously, both men fired. Shouts broke from the column, muzzles flashed, and bullets sang past. One of them hit the elephant in the ear, a sensitive spot. The beast trumpeted with rage. Eyes gleaming vengeance, trunk raised to strike, the elephant bore down on the running men. It caught up with them and plowed through, scattering bodies.

"Ayu!"

They thundered up the trail, leaving carnage in their wake: mangled bodies trampled to death, men smashed by the flailing trunk, men disemboweled by the ivory tusks. This was how elephants smashed columns of men when they were used in battle in the early days of Thailand.

But death also came to those who ran out of the way. Both sides of the trail were thick with *pungi* sticks, low ones for tripping a man, high ones to catch him full in the chest or back. As the Tiger soldiers dispersed into the undergrowth, they were impaled by the poisoned spikes. Behind Bolan the forest filled with screams of agony.

The forest lit up, and figures appeared holding flaming torches. They were the village women, and they held knives in their hands as well. Fleet of foot, as only mountain dwellers can be, they made their way between the *pungis* to finish off the soldiers and collect their weapons. The gruesome task had been left to the women because all available men were needed on the DZ. To help them, many women had brought their sons. The sons went about the business of human butchery with the nonchalant air of Idaho farmboys administering the coup de grace to fish.

"Ayu!"

They were reaching the head of the column. A white face went by, split in two by one of the swords. A rifle fired aimlessly before its owner exploded into a gory mess under the impact of the elephant's feet. Suddenly they were in the clear, the trail empty. The transition was startling: one moment the noise of battle, the next only the animal's thudding footsteps along a peaceful forest trail bathed in moonlight.

The mahout brought the elephant to a halt. Panting

wildly, mouth foaming, its entire body glistening with sweat, the elephant proceeded to fan its ears to cool itself.

The mahout came up to the howdah and lit a cigarette. "Big Bottom needs rest," he announced.

"Not too long," said Bolan. They had to get to the DZ.

"Two cigarettes," said the mahout, indicating the length of time they would stay there. He nodded in the direction of the forest. Rifle shots now punctuated the screams as the women, tired of killing by hand, killed the enemies with their rifles. "Tiger finished."

"Only a column," Bolan cautioned. "Lots more troops at the Tiger camp."

"We will finish them, too," said the mahout. "Then we go to fight Chinese in Yunnan." One of the Meo dreams was to reconquer their ancient homeland, southern China. There were still five million Meo living there.

A shot rang from inside the trees and the mahout toppled.

Fenster! The name exploded in Bolan's head as he recognized the sound of a Remington .306.

The elephant wheeled and with a trumpeting shriek charged into the trees. A figure detached itself from a tree—a tall figure with a white face—and fled inside the forest. Bolan held on to the howdah for dear life, crouching to avoid being decapitated by overhead branches. They barreled through the jungle, the elephant swerving, tearing vines and snapping trees in a cacophony of thrashing and trumpeting. Fenster was an agile runner and was outwitting the elephant by changing course at the last moment. But bit by bit the elephant gained.

The chase led into a clearing. The elephant was nearly on him when Fenster dived into a clump of bullaca bamboo. The elephant went after him, jabbing with its immense tusks, flailing its trunk. There was a scream, then the animal backed out with Fenster held firmly in its trunk. It backed all the way into the clearing and began swinging its prey from one side to the other. Bolan stood up in the howdah, and both men could see each other, Fenster sailing through the air as if on a swing, his eyes wide with fear, Bolan watching him, the Armalite in his hands.

"Help me!" Fenster cried. "Shoot him behind the ear!"

Bolan remained motionless, a figure in black bathed by the icy moonlight. Occasionally his silver collar glistened.

The elephant tossed the man high in the air. Fenster landed with a loud thud and began moaning.

The elephant went over and very gently placed a foot on Fenster to hold him while its trunk sought out an arm.

An agonizing scream escaped the man's lips as the animal tore off the arm and sent it flying through the air.

Then the beast proceeded to tear off the remaining limbs.

Finally, giving an ear-splitting shriek, it trampled the dismembered torso to a pulp.

A birdcall sounded from inside the trees, and the mahout appeared. Seeing him, the elephant gave a joyous cry and ran to meet him. It hoisted him gently with its trunk, and the mahout came to the howdah, a bloody hand clutching his shoulder.

"Bullet went through," he announced cheerfully.

"Let's take a look," said Bolan. He bared the mahout's shoulder and examined the wound by the light of a match.

The mahout nodded at the mess on the ground. "Who was he?"

"A bad man," said Bolan. He finished his examination and blew out the match. "On the way to the drop zone we will stop at the village. I want to bandage your wound."

"We will be late for parachuting," said the mahout.

"My mahout is more important," said Bolan.

The other grunted, pleased. To the elephant he said, *"Paj."* The beast moved off.

8

Flaming torches lighting their way, the handful of riders galloped in the night. A trail loomed ahead. The point rider swerved into it and the rest followed. The new trail led them out of the forest into a savanna, a plain of tall grass and woods. The torch riders swirled their torches to extinguish them, and the group rode on by the light of the moon, grass swishing under the horses' legs. The headman, who was leading, maintained a grueling pace. It was two hours past the scheduled drop time.

On the other side of the plain was a range of hills. Twenty minutes later they were spurring their ponies up the slopes, galloping until the ground became too steep, then continuing at a fast climb, the horses straining. They went over a ridge, down an incline, and up another slope. When they got to the top, they stopped.

Below lay the Valley of the Spirits, and the slope directly ahead was dark with people and horses...and they were still waiting.

"Colonel!" exclaimed Vang Ky. "Where are the planes?"

"Weather could have delayed them," said Bolan. "It happens."

"But the sky is clear."

"Yes, but over the ocean there might be a storm."

"Password!" called the voice. A group of men emerged from bushes holding crossbows.

The headman gave the password, and the men joined them. They were one of the teams Nark had posted on the ridges to guard the drop zone. There was always a danger some Tiger patrol might show up.

"A plane came, but it did not stop," said one of the guards.

"When?" asked the headman.

"A little after we arrive."

The headman looked questioningly at Bolan.

"Could have been an airliner," said Bolan. "We'll ask Nark."

They rode to a clump of trees midway down the slope that was to be the command post for the drop. In a clearing a campfire had been lit around which sat the other headmen and Nark. When he saw Bolan, the tall man with the mustache left the group and came over.

"How did it go?" he asked.

"Better than here," said Bolan, sensing the tension.

"There's talk of going home. Some people are saying the spirits are angry we disturbed them. I'm trying to keep them from leaving."

"What's this about a plane?"

"Wasn't ours," said Nark. "A jet fighter by the sound of it. Flew high."

Bolan dismounted and tied his horse to a tree. By the fire, Vang Ky was surrounded by angry headmen. *Poor Vang Ky,* thought Bolan, *always taking the flak.* "Let's take a walk," he said to Nark.

They left the trees and came out into the grassland. There were a good three thousand people on the slope and several hundred horses. An atmosphere of doom hung in the air, everyone conscious of what no drop signified. Instead of them attacking Tiger, Tiger would attack them, and this time the expedition would be accompanied by gunship helicopters. It would be a massacre.

Bolan and Nark sat down in the grass and lit cigarettes. For a while they watched the Montagnards. They stood like statues, their upturned faces watching the

HE'S EXPLOSIVE.
HE'S MACK BOLAN...
AGAINST ALL ODDS

He learned his deadly skills in Vietnam...then put them to good use by destroying the Mafia in a blazing one-man war. Now **Mack Bolan** is back to battle new threats to freedom—and he's recruited some high-powered forces to help...**Able Team**—Bolan's famous Death Squad from the Mafia wars—now reborn to tackle urban savagery too vicious for regular law enforcement. And **Phoenix Force**—five extraordinary warriors handpicked by Bolan to fight the dirtiest of anti-terrorist wars around the world.

Fight alongside these three courageous forces for freedom in all-new, pulse-pounding action-adventure novels! Travel to the jungles of South America, the scorching sands of the Sahara desert, and the desolate mountains of Turkey. And feel the pressure and excitement building page after page, with non-stop action that keeps you enthralled until the explosive conclusion! Yes, Mack Bolan and his combat teams are living large...and they'll fight against all odds to protect our way of life!

Now you can have all the new Executioner novels delivered right to your home!

You won't want to miss a single one of these exciting new action-adventures. And you don't have to! Just fill out and mail the card at right, and we'll enter your name in the Executioner home subscription plan. You'll then receive four brand-new action-packed books in the Executioner series every other month, delivered right to your home! You'll get two **Mack Bolan** novels, one **Able Team** book and one **Phoenix Force**. No need to worry about sellouts at the bookstore...you'll receive the latest books by mail as soon as they come off the presses. That's four enthralling action novels every other month, featuring all three of the exciting series included in the Executioner library. Mail the card today to start your adventure.

FREE! Mack Bolan bumper sticker.

When we receive your card we'll send your four explosive Executioner novels and, absolutely FREE, a Mack Bolan "Live Large" bumper sticker! This large, colorful bumper sticker will look great on your car, your bulletin board, or anywhere else you want people to know that you like to "live large." And you are under no obligation to buy anything—because your first four books come on a 10-day free trial! If you're not thrilled with these four exciting books, just return them to us and you'll owe nothing. The bumper sticker is yours to keep, FREE!

Don't miss a single one of these thrilling novels...mail the card now, while you're thinking about it. And get the Mack Bolan bumper sticker FREE as our gift!

HE'S UNSTOPPABLE. AND HE'LL FIGHT TO DEFEND FREEDOM!

FREE! MACK BOLAN BUMPER STICKER
when you join our home subscription plan.

Gold Eagle Reader Service, a Division of Worldwide Library
2504 W. Southern Avenue, Tempe AZ 85282

YES, please send me my first four Executioner novels, and include my FREE Mack Bolan bumper sticker as a gift. These first four books are mine to examine free for 10 days. If I am not entirely satisfied with these books, I will return them within 10 days and owe nothing. If I decide to keep these novels, I will pay just $1.95 per book (total $7.80). I will then receive the four new Executioner novels every other month as soon as they come off the presses, and will be billed the same low price of $7.80 per shipment. I understand that each shipment will contain two Mack Bolan novels, one Able Team and one Phoenix Force. There are no shipping and handling or any other hidden charges. I may cancel this arrangement at any time, and the bumper sticker is mine to keep as a FREE gift, even if I do not buy any additional books.

166-CIM-PACN

Name	(please print)	
Address		Apt No.
City	State	Zip
Signature	(If under 18, parent or guardian must sign.)	

This offer limited to one order per household. We reserve the right to exercise discretion in granting membership. If price changes are necessary, you will be notified. Offer expires December 31, 1984.

PRINTED IN U.S.A.

western horizon, the direction of the Indian Ocean. No one spoke, and the only sound was that of clothes flapping in the breeze.

"The wind's picking up," said Nark.

"Yeah," said Bolan. With the wind would come clouds, and clouds were bad for a drop. Planes had trouble finding the drop zone.

They stretched out and smoked in silence, eyes on the stars in the sky. "What are we going to do if the planes don't come, John?" asked Nark after a while.

"I don't know." Bolan sighed. "I really don't know." He felt tired, physically and emotionally.

"Avion!" someone shouted.

"Avion! Avion! Avion!" The cry spread until the whole slope was shouting it.

In the west, high in the sky, a light was moving. Bolan and Nark sprang to their feet. Another chance traveler, or for them? Nark took a flashlight from his pocket and they waited.

The light drew nearer, flying straight for them. All of a sudden it went out. A disappointed groan swept the slope. Suddenly there was a shout. The light came again, and now it was flashing. It was flashing short, short, long, short. The letter *F* in Morse.

"Foxtrot!" cried Nark.

"Reply," said Bolan calmly.

Nark pointed the flashlight at the plane and Morsed the letter *K,* the ground recognition signal. In the sky the light flashed *B,* the second half of the air recognition signal.

"He's seen us!" said Nark.

Bolan cupped his mouth. "Light the fires!"

The valley echoed the shout, and moments later flames licked piles of branches stacked at the start and end of the drop zone. The bonfires grew, bathing the valley in a warm, red glow, silhouetting the men and ponies.

A deep drone filled the sky. It grew rapidly, and a floatplane flew over the valley. An object fell and a parachute blossomed.

"I'll get it," said Nark, running down.

A couple of Montagnards helped him to detach a container from the billowing parachute, and he dragged it back to the slope. Its contents included two radio handsets. Bolan took one, Nark the other.

Bolan pulled out the aerial on his. "Phoenix to aircraft, do you read me?"

The set crashed with static. "Five on five," the voice in the sky replied. "Is the DZ secure? Got a passenger for you."

Bolan and Nark exchanged glances. "Send him down," said Bolan, intrigued.

They checked the rest of the goodies in the container. For Nark there was a camera; for Bolan there was a Makarov 9mm pistol with a silencer, and for both of them, money in three denominations—Thai bahts, Russian rubles, and U.S. dollars.

"What's the pistol for?" asked Nark.

"I'll find a use for it," said Bolan.

The floatplane came in. A parachutist sailed to the ground preceded by a container dangling from his leg at the end of a cord. Such a setup usually denoted a precious cargo, one from which the parachutist did not intend to be separated.

"Romeo one to Phoenix," said the floatplane's pilot. "As soon as the passenger is off the field we'll proceed with cargo drop. The other aircraft will be here in a minute."

"Copied," said Bolan.

On the field, the new arrival had collapsed his chute but seemed to be having a hard time extricating himself from his harness. Finally the harness fell away, and the man picked up the container and ran from the field, taking off his helmet.

"It's Harry Stressner," exclaimed Nark. "Harry, over here!" Nark waved. He turned to Bolan. "Harry's one of our communications men."

They watched him make his way up the slope, a big blond man in brown overalls. Bolan was sure this mystery visitor heralded new complications. From experience Bolan knew that when people turned up unexpectedly, it usually meant something was going wrong. Otherwise they would not have been sent. It cost money to send people on a mission.

"Hi, Nark," said Stressner, coming up to them. He nodded to Bolan. "Colonel."

"Good morning," said Bolan.

Just then the sky roared as the floatplane made its cargo drop. This time a whole string of parachutes bloomed. One of the containers sailed over a bonfire beyond the drop zone.

Bolan pressed the talk button on the radio. "You were a little long there, Romeo. Shorten your drop fifty."

"Sorry about that," replied the voice in the sky.

A new voice broke in. "Romeo one, this is Romeo two and three coming in. Delta Zulu in sight."

"Go right in, two and three," said the pilot.

Two lights were moving in the northern sky, approaching the valley in a wide arc. As they neared, the planes took shape, an Ilyushin and an Antonov boxcar, the same that brought Bolan to Thailand three days earlier. Like the arms, the planes for Galloping Horse were Russian. The floatplane was a Beriev. All three had been purchased on the black market in Angola, a Soviet client state in Africa.

The Antonov came in first, its silver fuselage shining in the moonlight. Halfway over the valley the pilot gunned the engines, and with a roaring thunderclap the aircraft shot skyward almost vertically. A string of crates flew out its back door, some with three parachutes attached to them. The crates landed with heavy thuds.

The camouflage-patterned Ilyushin followed. It flew low and slow, pushed off course by the wind. The Ilyushin did not have the benefit of a back door, and dispatchers, not gravity, had to do the work. They shoved container after container through both side doors so that two strings of parachutes seemed to follow the plane as it flew over.

The Beriev flew past again, the Soviet red star clearly visible on its white tail. The radio came to life. "Romeo to Phoenix. The container with the orange parachute is money. The striped green is medicine."

"Roger, Romeo," Bolan replied. "Let's take a break to clear the field." The drop zone was becoming crowded with equipment, and there was the danger of collision and damage. Bolan turned to a group of men and horses nearby. "Major Vang Ky."

The headman ran over. Bolan explained to him about the money. Vang Ky shouted orders to some men, and they ran onto the field. Bolan followed their progress, making sure the money container was picked up. Stories about covert missions were full of instances of money containers being lost, and of the people who were supposed to pick them up saying they never did.

The container retrieved, Bolan cupped his mouth. "Clear the field!"

A cheer broke from the slope as men ran down, pulling horses behind them. It was a race, a bit of fun after the tension and uncertainty of the night. Overhead, the planes began circling the valley in a holding pattern. Bolan turned to Stressner. It was time to find out what he was bringing.

"To what do we owe the pleasure?"

"The helicopter broke down, and they can't find Russian spare parts," Stressner announced. "The files will have to be transmitted out." He nodded at the container by his feet. "I brought a Crypton."

"A Crypton?" Bolan said.

"A high-speed key transmitter. Works like a typewriter. Codes itself."

"That'd take hours," said Bolan.

"Depends on how much there is to send," said Stressner.

Bolan nodded to himself. It meant an overhaul of their strategy. Galloping Horse had been planned as a hit and destroy operation, in and out. Now they would have to provide security after capturing the hardsite to make sure the transmitting was not interrupted by the appearance of some Tiger unit returning from the bush.

Furthermore, there was the agreement with the Meo. Nothing in it stipulated they had to establish a defensive perimeter after the hardsite was captured. Montagnards were loath to do that, hit and run being their specialty. He or Nark might be able to convince them to prolong their services, but they most certainly would ask for overtime money.

"I don't suppose Control sent some extra cash, did they?" asked Bolan.

"Beg your pardon, Colonel?" said Stressner.

"Never mind." Obviously they had not.

"We could offer them the gold at the hardsite," suggested Nark. He had caught on immediately to what Bolan was thinking.

"They already expect the gold," said Bolan.

"They might expect it, but nothing in the agreement we made with them stipulates they're entitled to it," said Nark. "I intentionally refrained from making any commitment."

Bolan chewed on a blade of grass. It was a moot point, but it was a start. In fact, it was about the only approach he could think of. "Okay, I'll try that."

"Romeo one to Phoenix. Can we resume?"

The last crate was being dragged off the field by ponies. "Go ahead, Romeo," said Bolan. He looked at Nark. "Take over," he said and set off for the woods to solve the latest problem.

IN THE FOREST, by the light of flaming torches, headmen were prying open crates and giving out arms. Others were demonstrating how to use them. A noisy crowd milled amid the trees, and the air resounded with the rattle of bolts and slamming magazines. There was also a great deal of brave war talk. Gloom had given way to bravado.

As he made his way through the crowd, Bolan observed the wide variety of weapons. There were brand-new Kalashnikovs and ancient Mosin-Nagants, Dragunov snipers, and Simonov carbines. There were several makes of machine and submachine guns, and four types of grenades: soup can, egg, pineapple, and potato masher.

The variety was something Bolan would have preferred to do without—the profusion of calibers meant ammunition was not interchangeable—but he had been warned to expect it. To avoid arousing interest that might have compromised the mission, the arms were bought in small quantities in various parts of the world, and not everyone had the same weapons for sale.

Bolan found Vang Ky by a crate of pepeshas, the acronym for the PPSH-41, the famed submachine gun of World War II whose perforated barrel and circular 70-round ammunition drum gave it a distinctive appearance. With it the Red Army drove the Germans from the Soviet Union. The guns had been bought in Chad from a supposed Marxist revolutionary making a killing from the resale of arms given to him by the Soviet Union.

"Everything going okay?" Bolan asked.

"Very good, Colonel," replied Vang Ky, his mood visibly improved. "The men are very happy. Plenty of guns."

"And the money?"

"Already divided."

Bolan watched him explain to a younger man how to use the pepesha.

As with most older Montagnards, Vang Ky was familiar with World War II Russian weaponry from the war fought from 1946 to 1954 between the Vietminh and the French in which the Montagnards sided with the French.

When Vang Ky finished, Bolan asked, "Can I have a word with you in private?"

"Important?"

"Yes."

The headman signaled to an assistant to take over, and they went back out onto the field. A plane was coming in for a drop. Bolan waited until the plane passed and the noise subsided, then he explained the problem and made his proposition. In return for a defensive follow-up, the Meo could have the Tiger gold.

Vang Ky considered it for a while, eyes on the ground, teeth sucking the air. Bit by bit his head began shaking. "No, Colonel," he said finally. "No good. If we must defend, we must be paid more. And not with gold. The gold belongs to the Hmong."

"Not quite," said Bolan.

For the next quarter of an hour they haggled like a couple of fishmongers. It was a role Bolan did not relish, but he did not shirk it. As Bismarck once observed, three things are necessary to win a war: money, money, and money. And he who talks money by necessity talks like a fishmonger.

"Okay, Major," he said at last, "if that's how you feel, you can lead the attack yourself. Nark and I are pulling out."

The headman started, taken aback. A ruse or for real? He was well aware the Meo needed Bolan as much as Bolan needed the Meo. Without Bolan, the chances of them destroying Tiger were nil. Instead, Tiger would destroy the Meo. "Pull out?" he exclaimed. "You cannot do that!"

"You don't think so?" said Bolan. "Listen, Major, the whole point of attacking Tiger is to exploit their files. Without security they can't be transmitted. The attack becomes pointless."

Again Vang Ky lowered his eyes and sucked through his teeth. Again, his head began to shake. "No, Colonel, I still cannot agree."

"*Sombaj,* Major," said Bolan and walked off.

"Wait!" Vang Ky called after him. He ran up to Bolan's side. "Let us say I agree. Could you obtain immigration visas for my sons?"

Bolan stared down at him in amazement. *You son of a gun,* he said to himself. *Talk about a horse trader.* All the while Vang Ky had been building up to this. "That could be arranged," he said.

"Then I agree. A defensive perimeter in return for the gold. And visas for my sons. Shake?"

They shook hands, and Bolan went back to Nark.

"Well?" asked Nark.

"We're back on the rails," said Bolan.

"I knew you'd do it."

"Romeo one to Phoenix!" The voice was frantic. "Low-flying aircraft closing in from the south. Unidentified."

"I thought those gizmos were supposed to blind their radar," said a voice in one of the planes.

"Goddamned Russian equipment," spat another.

From over the ridge came the sound of jets. Two F-86 Sabre fighters roared over the valley, and Bolan caught sight of red-white-and-blue rondelles: Royal Thai Air Force. The planes banked and went into a tight circle over the valley, effectively blocking any further drops.

"Romeo one to Phoenix. Fighters demanding we identify. What do we tell 'em?"

"Stall them," Bolan replied. "You don't understand. *Ne panimaiyu*. In the meantime, what is status of cargo? Romeo one?"

"Clear."

"Romeo two?"

"Clear."

"Romeo three?"

"We still have to drop the mortar," replied the pilot of the Ilyushin.

"Got to have that," said Nark to Bolan.

"Not if it's going to cost us a crew, we don't," Bolan told him. "The moment he tries to make an approach, they'll shoot." Bolan jabbed the talk button. "Okay, guys, we'll forego the mortar. Prepare to split."

"Romeo one to Phoenix!" The voice was frantic again. "We're ordered to proceed to Oudon."

"Keep saying you don't understand in Russian and stand by."

Bolan slung the radio over his shoulder and ran for the woods. He grabbed a Degtyarev machine gun, inserted a drum of ammunition, and ran out. He climbed the slope to a rocky tower and took up a position in the entrance to a cave, gun at his hip.

The Sabres were curving toward him, coming from the left. They went out of sight, and he heard them fly past behind him. They reappeared on his right, exhaust glowing. They curved once more and straightened out over the opposite ridge.

Bolan pulled the trigger and a line of tracers arched over the valley. The rounds came nowhere near the planes, but Bolan was not interested in hitting them; he only wanted to attract their attention. And attract it he did. The fighters zoomed and peeled. Two Immelmann turns followed, and they came shrieking down at him.

"Split, Romeo!" Bolan shouted into the radio. "Split!"

The nose of one of the fighters winked, and colored

tracers from its cannon flew at him. Bolan stepped into the cave. It was a trick he picked up from the VC though they, he had to admit, were much more sophisticated. The VC pulled the stunt using artillery.

The rocky tower thudded under the impact of the projectiles. The planes roared over, and a bomb exploded outside. The ground shook, the cave blurred. A section of the wall collapsed, and the cave filled with dust.

Bolan ran out, coughing. There was a crater ten yards from the tower. As for the planes, they were banking, coming out of their dive. One left the valley, heading after a plane, the other prepared to pay Bolan another visit.

Bolan teased it with a burst and stepped inside. Once again, the tower thudded. Another bomb exploded. As it did so, the entrance of the cave flashed white and a blast of hot air swept the inside. Close!

Bolan ran out and tumbled headfirst into a crater just outside the entrance. As he was scrambling from it, the radio came on. Over the crash of static a voice was shouting.

"Fighter on your tail! Fighter on your tail! Look out!"

"Oh, shit," a voice said calmly. In the northern sky something flashed.

"Fire! Fire! We're burning! We're hit!"

"Pipe down," the calm voice told him. "Damage report."

"Fire in number four engine. Fuel pressure dropping."

"Phoenix to aircraft on fire," said Bolan into his set. "Can you make it back to land here?"

"We'll try," the calm voice replied. "Thanks for the invitation."

The sound of cannon in the sky sent Bolan diving into the crater. The Sabre roared over, the rocky tower flashed as if hit by lightning, the ground shook, rocks and dirt rained on Bolan.

When he finally got up, the tower was no more. Nor was the cave. Had Bolan gone back into the cave for the third time, he would be climbing the ladder to heaven, as the Meo put it so poetically.

A drone filled the sky, the Ilyushin was returning. From its starboard wing trailed two tongues of flame. Both engines were now on fire. On the field, Nark was supervising the clearing of the drop zone. The last crates were being dragged off by teams of ponies. Bolan scanned the sky for the fighters, but they were gone. Gone to refuel, which meant others would be coming.

"Romeo three to Phoenix," said the voice in the sky. "We're coming in."

The Ilyushin approached, one of its two remaining engines coughing. Then both fell silent. The plane lost height rapidly. It flew over the first bonfire, and Bolan could hear the rush of air and the noise of flames sounding like flapping cloth. The silver fuselage gleamed red from the bonfires. The landing gear was not extended. The plane touched down and with a crunching noise slid on its belly, raising a cloud of dust. It plowed through the second bonfire, a wing tipped, and it spun to a halt.

The crew jumped out but instead of getting away proceeded to unload. Nark and Stressner ran to them with Montagnards coming after, leading ponies. Bolan followed. By the time he reached the plane, the mortar tubes and bombs had been unloaded. Everyone grabbed something and ran.

"Avion!"

From the south another pair of fighters was streaking toward them. This time the whole valley opened up. The air filled with the crash of automatic weapons and a panoply of tracers formed the sky. The planes peeled, avoiding the tracers.

"Cease fire!" Bolan shouted, running along the slope. "Cease fire!" The last thing he wanted was to shoot down a Thai plane. They were fighting Tiger Enterprises, not Thailand.

The shooting died down while the Thunderstreaks circled the valley by a wide margin. Nark came running to Bolan. "They'll have bombers with napalm here in a moment."

"And heliborne troops first thing in the morning," Bolan added. "Major Vang Ky!"

The headman ran to him up the slope.

"Move out," Bolan told him.

"For village?"

"No, we go directly to the Tiger camp."

He nodded and ran off.

Whistles blew, voices shouted. Bolan's Montagnard army was finally on the march.

9

By noon they had covered a third of the way. They were in the La Kon forest, famed for its sandalwood and its herds of wild elephants. It was there that Bolan called a long halt, the first of their journey. The trees provided plenty of shade from the now broiling sun and there was a stream. The Montagnards watered the horses, Bolan posted guards, and the men sat to eat. It was simple Montagnard fare, glutinous rice dipped in pimento, washed down with water from the stream, which they drank in cups made from banana leaves. Lunch over, everyone stretched out for some shut-eye except for the whites who were not used to siestas. They sat in a group talking. Nark was describing how the Thais fought the heroin trade.

"One day the district chief came to see me and said they had captured a ton of raw opium. He said they were going to burn it. Why didn't I get some American reporters to come up? I called the DEA office in Bangkok, and they sent a busload. The office liked the publicity. It shows Congress back home what a good job we're doing. The district chief put on a big party with girls and dancing, the reporters took pictures, and I paid out the reward money. In those days we paid reward money. Only later did I learn that what we burned was silage. The opium had been resold to a merchant in Bangkok. Clever, no?"

"Why are they like that?" asked Heath, the Ilyushin pilot. "Don't they care what that stuff does to the people in America?"

"America?" said Nark. "They don't give a damn about America. All those Thai politicians care about is themselves. Tiger pays protection money to Bangkok. Without it a lot of those government people wouldn't be able to afford their villas and their Mercedes. So they play ball.

"Mind you," Nark went on, "there's also economics. If Bangkok put Tiger out of business, the opium farmers wouldn't have anyone to sell to. How would they make a living? Bangkok's afraid they'd turn Communist. USAID suggested schemes for substitute crops. Trouble is there isn't much demand for substitute crops from the Triangle. The area's too far from the main markets. Anyway, the farmers prefer opium; it's more profitable."

A whistling hoot traveled from afar. Bolan's brow furrowed. "What's that?"

"A railroad runs through the forest," Nark explained. "Trains carry ore and lumber from mines and sawmills up north. The maps don't show it. The line was laid down only recently. Guess who owns the railroad?"

"Don't tell me," said Bolan.

"You guessed," said Nark.

"Who owns it?" asked Heath.

"Tiger, of course," said Nark. "In the Golden Triangle there's hardly anything they don't own. Which is why they've got so much clout with the Thais. They've got the money and they've got the troops. Some people call this a second Taiwan, another Nationalist Chinese republic. Unofficial, of course." He paused to listen to the distant whistling. "Must be a lot of elephants on the line."

"Avion!"

The shout sent Bolan and Nark to their feet. A rapidly approaching drone grew in the sky, and a small plane skimmed the treetops. "Thai army," said Nark, catching the Pali writing on the fuselage.

"And he's coming back," said Nark, ears registering a change in the pitch of the engine. "Everyone under the trees!" he shouted.

It was easier said than done. The noise of the Piper Cub had sent the horses galloping in confusion. The Montagnards were still chasing after them when the spotter made its second pass.

"Now he knows we're here for sure," said Nark.

Vang Ky ran to them. "Colonel, we've been discovered!" he cried. "What do we do?"

"Round up the horses for a start," Bolan replied, anger in his voice. "I told you to tie them."

"I'm sorry, Colonel. I tried to tell them."

Discipline was not one of the Montagnards' strong points. Everyone did what he wanted, individualism and personal freedom being enshrined traditions. There was not much Bolan could do about that, either. With irregular troops you could not play the disciplinarian; the troops simply went home.

"He must have glided down," said Heath, "or we'd have heard him earlier. It's almost as if he knew we were here."

"He probably did, too," said Bolan, eyes on the circling spotter.

"How could he know?"

"By the color of the trail."

"Sorry?"

"An unused trail's yellow," Bolan explained, "the ground bleached by the sun. When a lot of men march on a trail they churn the ground back to its original color, terra-cotta. A good spotter will look out for that."

The headman Ly appeared. "Colonel, we must do something," he said. "The Thais will send troops and will block the trail."

Bolan nodded, eyes still following the spotter. The plane was unarmed, but that was small consolation. "Nark! Bring the map."

They laid the map flat on the ground and Bolan studied it. There were two ways out of the forest: north by the trail and east by a dirt road.

"Does this road still exist?" asked Bolan.

"Yes," replied Vang Ky. "But we want to go north. Tiger is to the north."

"I know," said Bolan, "but I propose to give the Thais the idea we're changing directions. I want them to think we're going east. Then, while the Thais are looking for us in the east, we disappear to the north."

"How can we do this?" asked Ly.

Bolan told him.

A LITTLE LATER fifty Montagnard riders slipped from the main force, heading east. They left in groups of five, keeping close to the trees—away from openings in the canopy—so the Piper would not spot them. All carried machetes in addition to their weapons.

At their head rode Bolan and Heath. The pilot came from New Mexico and was at home in the saddle. Bolan had taken a liking to him; the young man impressed him. *He brings back a burning plane, lands, and instead of running, starts unloading. Cool.*

The forest was flat, so they made good time. They came to the dirt road and followed parallel to it, keeping inside the trees. The road crossed the rail line, and eventually they reached the eastern edge of the woods. Ahead was a stretch of open country before the road disappeared into another forest.

They all dismounted, and the Montagnards proceeded to cut down branches that they tied into large bunches using lianas. Bolan inspected the road. The soil was powder dry; there had been no rain since the night after he arrived in Thailand. Perfect.

When everything was ready, Bolan inspected the diversion force. They sat on their horses, rifles on their laps, handkerchiefs over their noses like bandits. Behind each horse was a large bundle of branches attached by a cord to the saddle.

"Remember," Bolan told them, "when you shoot, you shoot to miss. If we down that plane, the Thais will send a regiment and we'll never get out."

Grunts acknowledged this last point.

They checked their radios. Twenty handsets arrived with the arms. Communications always played a big part in Bolan's scheme of things. Then Bolan ran to a spot from which he could observe the entire road.

"Okay, Heath, let's go!" Bolan said into his radio.

A pair of riders galloped out of the forest, down the road and into the next forest, the branches behind them raising dust. The dust hung in midair, as there was hardly any wind.

"Next," said Bolan.

A second pair galloped out, this one already partly obscured by the dust. As they went by, the cloud over the road thickened.

"Next."

On the fifth turn, Nark's voice came on the radio. "It's working," he said. "The Piper's heading your way."

The spotter flew overhead. A wing dipped as the pilot prepared to investigate this dust cloud to the east. A moment later he was zooming skyward, bracketed by tracers from riders on the road and in the forests. When he reached a safe height he began circling.

"Phoenix to Nark," Bolan said into the radio. "He's hooked. Start moving out."

"On the way," the other replied.

Now began a tense waiting game, the plane circling, the riders galloping. Occasionally the plane tried to come down for a closer look. And each time it was driven off by gunfire. A closer inspection might have revealed riders galloping both ways.

The radio came to life. It was Nark. "We hear choppers.'' A little later he added, "Eight helicopters. Heading your way.''

The sky filled with the sound of rotor blades, and the helicopters passed over Bolan's head. They were Sikorskys. They flew far over the forest, the sound faded, and Bolan lost them from view. The plane went on circling, the riders galloped.

"Colonel," the radio whispered. "This is Ly in the other forest. I can hear the helicopters land. They are using the clearing. There is a big clearing in the middle." A little later, "The helicopters are leaving."

The Sikorskys reappeared over the forest, flying south this time. In due course the Piper flew off after them and a silence descended on the area. Bolan watched the Piper turn into a dot in the sky.

"Phoenix to Mr. Ly," said Bolan into the radio. "Return."

"Yes, sir."

"Phoenix to Nark. Where are you?"

"Couple of klicks from the northern edge," Nark replied. "But Major Vang Ky is already at the edge with the point team."

"Phoenix to Major Vang Ky. What's the terrain like?"

"Open land for five hundred yards, Colonel. And another forest. You want us to cross?"

"Wait until the main force reaches you," replied Bolan. "Then we all make a quick dash. The plane could return. Phoenix to Nark. When you cross, keep off the trail."

"Roger."

Bolan ran back to his riders. They presented quite a spectacle, men and horses covered in a thick layer of dust.

"Well done, brothers," said Bolan. "We tricked them."

Just then, however, the radio blared: "Nark to Phoenix. Urgent! Helicopters in the west. Flying north. Major Vang Ky, do you see them?"

"I see them, Mr. Nark, I see them. Many helicopters. One, two, three, four, five, six. And two more. Eight helicopter Mr. Nark. They are Hueys. They are flying for the next forest.... They are over the forest...I see ropes coming from them. Men are sliding down the ropes. Many men, Mr. Nark. Colonel, our way is blocked. What are we going to do?"

"Stand by," said Bolan. He took out a pack of cigarettes, lit one, then sat down by the foot of a tree.

"I guess we didn't trick them after all," said Heath.

"I guess not," said Bolan. He tilted his head back and closed his eyes. "Now we're in a real fix," he said quietly.

THE FOREST WAS BATHED in a hot afternoon stillness. Butterflies flew about and somewhere an insect buzzed. By the foot of the tree, Bolan went on smoking, head tilted, eyes closed. The mounted Montagnards watched with sympathy. It is at such moments soldiers are glad they are not the officer.

"Suppose we backtracked," suggested Heath. He squatted by Bolan's side. "We could take another trail."

"There are no other trails for miles," said Bolan without opening his eyes.

"Couldn't we go cross-country?"

"Take too long. We have to attack tonight."

A hooting whistle sounded from afar. Another train.

"Perhaps we can bribe our way out," suggested Heath. "A guy I know did that in Nam. Took a whole platoon through VC lines. Cost him a hundred bucks."

"That's because he only had a platoon. We're too many."

"Then let's shoot our way through."

"Not allowed to shoot Thais. Thailand is part of SEATO."

"I give up."

Bolan smiled, his eyes still shut. "Don't. Two minds are better than one." How the hell was he going to get his men past the Thais? They fell silent, listening to the buzz of the insects. In the distance the train kept hooting.

Bolan knew there was a way; there was always a way if you were prepared to make the necessary mental effort. Who would have thought one man could ambush two hundred? Well, it happened. How? Because he had imagined ambushing them with an elephant.

Think, think, he told himself. *Every riddle has an answer, every lock a key. All it takes is imagination....*

The train kept hooting and.... "The train!" Bolan sprang to his feet and raced for his horse. *"Paj!"* he shouted to his men, swinging into the saddle.

They charged headlong through the forest, Bolan ignoring the thorns tearing at his clothes, the branches whipping his face. Eyes filled with water from the rush of air, he led them crashing through the undergrowth, all his being concentrated on one thought: he had to get the train.

The whistling neared. The train was coming from the south. Soon he could hear the puffing of a steam locomotive. Then, as the locomotive passed ahead of him on the other side of some trees, he could hear the rumble of wheels.

The trees thinned and he saw it: a long line of ore and flatcars. The cars were empty. Perfect.

They rode out of the trees and galloped single file along the side of the track, heading after the locomotive, overtaking the cars one by one. The train moved slowly, as there were many cars and only one locomotive.

A passenger car appeared, the fourth car behind the

engine. As he galloped past it Bolan looked up and got a shock. The car was full of troops, and their fatigue caps told him the troops were Tiger. He saw them stare at him with surprise, and then he was past them.

But they quickly recovered; as he was nearing the engine he heard gunfire. The soldiers were engaging the Montagnards. Bolan turned in the saddle and waved to his men to disperse. They veered off and rode back into the trees. Now only Heath was with him.

Bolan passed a flatcar carrying Tiger horses and drew even with the locomotive. He took out his Makarov, grabbed the handrail, and swung himself into the cab. The pistol spat flame twice, and the two soldiers riding escort crumpled to the floor. The locomotive engineer backed against the controls in terror at the sight of this long nose in Montagnard dress, complete with silver collar.

"Stop the engines!" Bolan shouted above the noise of the wheels and the steam.

But the engineer did not react. He seemed paralyzed.

"I'll do it," said Heath. He shouted that he was the son of a railroad man and had ridden in locomotives. He shut the throttle, and the noise level in the cab fell by half. He took hold of the brake handle. "Hold tight!" he said, swinging the brake lever to Emergency.

Bolan grabbed the side of the cab as the locomotive lurched. The air filled with the sound of screaming metal, and they slid on the track, wheels locked. Finally, with another lurch, the whole train came to a sudden stop.

For a moment there was silence, broken only by the hiss of steam. Then they heard voices and boots running along the track. Bolan holstered the Makarov and unslung the AK-74 from his back. He had time to cock before the first Tiger soldiers appeared. He fired, two men fell, and the rest backed away.

"Reverse!" Bolan shouted.

Heath took the reverse lever and pulled, but it would not move. Just then the engineer came out of his dazed paralysis. He gave the lever an expert tug and it fell into position. They could go backward.

"Paj?" he asked.

"Paj! Paj!" Bolan shouted, firing through the side door to keep the troops at bay.

A pair of feet crunched on top of the coal tender. A muzzle flashed and something hot flew past Bolan's ear. A Simonov carbine barked as Heath fired, and a dead Tiger soldier fell headlong into the cab.

The engineer opened the throttle, steam left the engine stack loudly, and the forest began gliding past in reverse. From inside the trees muzzles flashed as Montagnard riders opened up on Tiger troops. A bullet clanged against the cab.

Bolan reached for his radio. "Mr. Ly, stop firing!" he shouted. "Cease fire!" All it would take was one bullet through the tank and they would be immobilized.

The train picked up speed, Bolan firing all the time. Now Heath too was firing, crouched by the opposite side door, shooting at Tiger soldiers in the grass who had tried to outflank them from the other side. On Bolan's side, men were running to rejoin the train. Bolan mowed them down.

The train rolled back from the danger zone. "Okay, Mr. Ly, you can resume shooting," Bolan told him by radio. "Try capturing some men so we can interrogate."

"We will try, Colonel," the headman replied. "Many Tiger soldiers are still in the passenger car." Suddenly his voice turned frantic. "Look out, Colonel! They are coming from the top of the car!"

Bolan scrambled up the coal tender. A line of men was emerging from a trapdoor. Some were walking along the roof, others were sliding down into one of the flatcars that separated the passenger car from the loco-motive.

Bolan changed magazines and began firing. Men fell off the roof to the side of the track, some under the wheels of cars. Two managed to get back into the carriage. The trapdoor shut.

"Nark to Phoenix. Nark to Phoenix," the radio blared. "What's going on?"

"We have captured a train," Bolan answered. "There are flatcars for horses and more cars for men. We are going out by train."

"You're kidding!"

"I'm on it right now," said Bolan. He explained about the troops. "We've got to keep moving so they can't come out of the passenger car and swamp us." Then he told him what he wanted done. "Signal when you're in position. Out."

For the next hour the train went up and down the line, Bolan lying on top of the coal tender. The spot was a good observation post. He could thwart any new attempts by Tiger to attack him from the roof or, when they stopped to reverse direction, from the ground. It also enabled him to see when the train was approaching the end of the forest so he could reverse before they came out in the open. In the grassland they would be vulnerable to spotting by aircraft from far away. Finally he could look out for elephants on the tracks. From the engineer he had learned they were responsible for several derailments.

The radio came to life. It was Nark. "We're at the track. I'm positioning the men. Got interesting information about the Tiger troops. They're escorting wages to the hardsite. Ly got that from captured prisoners. Are you rolling south or north?"

"North," Bolan replied.

"When the train comes in sight, I'll go on the track and wave."

"I'll be watching for you."

A few minutes later, through the smoke and steam, Bolan caught sight of Nark far down the line, waving his arms. Bolan leaned down and told the engineer to reduce speed. Now came the tricky part. The train had to stop so that Nark's assault party was directly in front of the passenger car; otherwise men would be shooting at an angle and might hit the locomotive.

"You're stopping too early," Nark said on the radio.

Bolan slid down the coal into the cab. "Release brakes."

The engineer swung the brake lever to the open position, and the train picked up speed by a fraction. To come to a stop at an exact point would not be easy. Although they were rolling quite slowly, the number of cars gave them a lot of momentum.

"Good, good," Nark was saying. "Slow down again."

"Apply brakes," Bolan said.

"A little more, a little more," Nark went on. "Here we go. Three, two, one . . . zero!"

"Stop!" ordered Bolan.

The locomotive slid to a lurching stop. A moment of hissing silence followed, then the forest exploded with gunfire. Bolan pulled the engineer down, and all three crouched in the cab. Even with the best of plans, there were such things as stray bullets.

For over a minute the Montagnards poured fire into the passenger car from one side of the track, while on the other, a specially positioned machine gun sprayed the windows and doors every time someone tried to get out that way.

Over the gunfire Bolan could hear slamming magazines and clearing bolts. It was like being on a firing range.

Finally there was silence. Bolan imagined the Montagnards approaching the passenger car. A solitary burst fired, glass tinkled, and...silence. There was the sound of running feet along the track, then Nark climbed into the cab.

"They've surrendered," he announced.

"Good," said Bolan, lifting himself to his feet. "Let's load."

10

It was sunset when they finally steamed out of the forest. It had taken over two hours to load. First, ramps had to be built to get the horses onto the flatcars, then platforms had to be installed to turn the ore wagons into two-story cars, which doubled their capacity. In each car the floor was taken up by men and equipment. Over their heads was a bamboo platform on which stood more men. Even with these additions, however, they were short of space, and men had to sit on the locomotive, the passenger car roof, between the legs of horses, on couplings, and some hung from outside ladders.

"Colonel Phoenix's war train," Nark joked.

"Some war train," said Bolan. "We look more like an army in retreat."

They stood on top of the coal tender of the moving train surveying the long line of overcrowded cars. The car directly behind them was a flatcar with horses and men, then came two ore wagons full of men bristling with guns, then the passenger car with its rooftop passengers, then more ore wagons interspersed with flatcars. Over fifty cars.

They chugged at ten miles an hour through the savanna toward the next forest, trailing a pall of smoke, the machinist whistling nonstop to scare off elephants. Herds were crossing the line on their way to the evening watering, kicking up dust colored pink by the setting sun. The sun hung in the western sky over a ridge, a flaming disk.

"Isn't it beautiful!" said Nark, looking in the direction of the setting sun.

Bolan nodded, feasting his eyes on the sight. *When men roll to war, everything that represents life takes on added meaning,* he reflected. For him, a sense of added meaning was always present, for he was forever rolling to war. For him, the meaning was justice by fire.

"How soon do you figure we'll be in Py Fung?" asked Nark.

"If everything goes well, two hours," replied Bolan. "Then another three by trail. We should be in position, ready to attack, before midnight."

"What about the train?"

"We'll park it in a siding. The engine driver says there's enough canopy to hide it. We'll put a bullet through the tank so he can't report us. He'll have to walk to town."

"You told him?"

Bolan nodded. "I'm paying him a thousand bahts for the inconvenience."

They steamed into the next forest. It got darker and cooler, and in the confined space the wheels seemed much louder. Bolan's stomach tightened. The two hours it took them to load would have given the Thais plenty of time to put troops on the line as well. Bolan glanced behind him. The men in the ore wagons stood by the sides, guns pointing at the bordering forest. Bolan raised the radio to his mouth.

"This is the colonel speaking. All headmen, please remind your troops of the orders. We are not to fire on Thai troops even if they fire on us. I repeat: *we do not fire back*, even if we take casualties. Out."

"I don't think we have to worry too much on that score," said Nark. "While we were loading I heard the headmen telling their men that if anybody shot at the Thais they'd have their wages confiscated. I get the impression they realize your order is as much to their benefit as ours. When this mission's over, you and I will leave, but they have to go on living with the Thais. It's better not to rub your neighbor the wrong way too much.''

"Let's hope you're right," said Bolan.

The fear of a firefight with the Thais was a constant worry to Bolan. From experience he knew that fire control is one of the hardest orders for troops to follow. When bullets fly and men around you fall, it takes real discipline to resist firing back.

On this mission Bolan felt like a trapeze artist who has to perform two tricks at once. He had to destroy Tiger without killing any Thais who got in the way, a frustrating position for a commander to be in.

The president had told him, ''Your hands will be tied from the very start. If under the circumstances you prefer not to undertake the mission, I'll understand and we'll abandon it.'' But Bolan had a personal reason for wanting to destroy Tiger. It was another snaking head of the very same Hydra that had almost devoured Bolan's warriors off Cuba. He would fight for sure.

The train rounded a bend, and Bolan's fears materialized. The Thais *had* thought of putting troops on the rail line. On the track ahead burned red flares. Two soldiers stood by them, signaling with their arms for the train to stop. A group of four more stood to the side observing, one of them with a radio on his back. They all wore camouflage berets and were armed with CAR-15s. Thai rangers, the elite.

The engineer poked his head from the cab. ''We stop?'' he asked.

"Keep going!" Bolan shouted back. *"Paj!"*

The engineer began hooting, and the two soldiers stepped off the track. Bolan kept his eyes on their hands. But neither they nor the others made any attempt to bring up their weapons. They merely stood there watching, interested spectators, their stance relaxed, seemingly unconcerned that the train took no notice of their order.

As the train neared the group, Bolan saw one of them—an officer, judging by his side arm—motion to the radioman to pass him the telephone-like headset. He was speaking into it when the locomotive passed, his eyes on Bolan, his expression calm, unperturbed, professional.

"What was *that*?" Nark exclaimed.

"I don't know," said Bolan, turning to see what would happen next. But nothing happened. The Thais watched the cars roll by with the same detached air, the officer talking calmly into his set. Bolan lost them from view behind a bend. "They look like men who have something up their sleeve."

"What do you think it could be?" asked Nark.

"We'll discover soon enough," replied Bolan.

"You know, those were rangers."

"I know."

"Trained by our Green Berets."

"That should make things even more interesting."

They rolled through the forest, listening to the locomotive's puffing and the rumbling of the wheels, waiting for the evening's surprises. The air was getting darker, the trees so close to the track it was like going through a tunnel. Often they had to duck to avoid branches.

Finally they rounded a bend and steamed out into a large clearing. It was a good two miles long and a half mile wide. The track ran straight as an arrow, and in the distance more flares burned on the line. But it was not the flares that commanded Bolan's attention, it was the goings-on beyond them.

Fifty-or-so yards on the other side of the flares—it was hard to tell at that distance—men crouched over the track. And five hundred yards beyond them was another group. At the sight of the train, both rose and ran to join a third group, this one standing halfway between the track and the tree line. A man in the third group had a radio antenna protruding from his back.

In the split second it took him to register the scene, Bolan had the answer to what the Thais had up their sleeve. Having been informed by the others by radio that the train refused to stop, this group had mined the track. Bolan's experienced eye even told him how they had mined it: they had used the Fog Signal system.

Beyond the flares—the last warning to the train—a detonator lay on the track. When the wheels of the train crossed it, it would explode the charges down the line, the distance between the detonator and the charges giving the driver time to stop. The Fog Signal was used to stop a train by blowing up the track without derailing the train.

To Bolan it was obvious that the Thais, too, wanted to avoid bloodshed. The peace-loving Thais were practicing what they preached. But Bolan had a mission to carry out, a mission into which he had sunk a lot of time, effort, and pain. A man whose balls have been broiled does not give up at the last moment. Colonel Phoenix's war train was stopping for no one, bad guys or good.

"Give me smoke!" he shouted.

He leaped off the coal tender, landing on the flatcar amid men and horses. He swung into a saddle and dug in his heels. The horse leaped from the moving car. It landed, stumbled, recovered, and Bolan sent it galloping down the side of the train.

They passed the locomotive and began outdistancing it, heading for the flares. Tracers flew at him as the Thais opened fire. Almost immediately, however, the three mortar tubes on the gun platform opened up, and smoke bombs began exploding, creating a smoke screen between him and the Thais.

The screen advanced with him, the mortar crews loading as fast as the bombs left the tubes. But gaps between the screen were unavoidable, and Bolan's white horse stood out. Colored projectiles still sang past him.

They galloped past the spewing flares, and Bolan leaned in the saddle, eyes scanning the rail, searching for the watch-and-strap shape of the Fog Signal detonator. Suddenly, he was flying, catapulted over his horse that now had blood pouring from its head, shot.

He scrambled to his feet and began running. Bullets no longer sang past him, his Montagnard suit making him harder to see, but now he was conscious of a more ominous sound—the locomotive was catching up with him. Then he saw it, a black object against the shining rail.

Lungs bursting from the strain, eyes tearing from the rush of air, the smoke screen blowing in his direction, he raced for the detonator. He reached it, his hands sought out the detonator cord and he pulled. But the cord refused to budge. It was firmly attached to the rail by tape.

A whistle rent the air, the engine driver warning Bolan to get out of the way. A picture flashed before Bolan's eyes: himself with bandaged wrists, hands amputated by the locomotive's wheels. He wanted to run, but the bigger part of him—Bolan the professional—maintained his grip on the cord.

A piercing cry escaped his lips, a cry of controlled hysteria of the kind that gives enough strength to a woman to lift a car to save her child, and he threw himself backward to escape the thundering wheels. The cord came away with him.

The locomotive rolled past Bolan in a deafening cacophony of pistons, steam and wheels. The ground trembled, he felt metal heat, smelled grease. He scrambled to his feet and ran after the train.

As he ran he was conscious of stretching arms and

shouting mouths, but in a vague way, as if in a dream. Then his hands came into contact with metal, a metal ladder running up the side of an ore wagon. He grabbed it and was dragged along the ground, then he pulled himself up and began climbing. His head swam, and his body grew weak.

Scores of hands reached down for him. He felt himself lifted and pulled in over the side. At that moment a loud cheer went up from the train, but he did not hear it. Bolan's world had gone black.

11

Flanked by Nark and Vang Ky, Bolan surveyed the hardsite from the ridge he and Nark had been on before. It was a little after 2200 hours, and Bolan's Montagnard army was ready for battle. But so was Tiger, and that was the problem. The camp had been reinforced. A quartet of newly arrived Apache helicopters sat on the landing zone, the parade ground was a sea of troop tents, and fresh gun emplacements were in evidence everywhere.

"We will be massacred," said Vang Ky.

"If we follow our original plan, yes," said Bolan.

"You have another?"

"The colonel is thinking of walking in," said Nark.

"Walking in?" exclaimed Vang Ky.

"As Tiger," said Bolan. "As victorious Tiger." He looked at Nark. "Did you bring the uniforms?"

"Uniforms, weapons and bodies," Nark replied.

By 2300 hours the commandos were ready. He inspected them by moonlight as they stood in a forest clearing. There were two groups of men. The first was made up of forty Montagnards in uniforms of Tiger soldiers captured or killed in the battle of the train. They also carried Tiger weapons.

Bolan's plan was to gain entry into the hardsite by impersonating the returning Tiger party. But forty men were not enough to hold back the enemy while keeping the gates open for the rest of the force. Bolan needed at least twice that number. So he had contrived the idea of doubling his force with prisoners.

They formed the second group of the commando, men in regular Montagnard dress with bound wrists and cords around their necks, both lightly tied so they could get free in a hurry. The armament for this group was in sacks on horses that would be led by the soldiers, ostensibly captured weapons. Some men were bandaged to look wounded.

The inspection over, Bolan signaled to the men to assemble around him. "You look very realistic," he told them. "We should have no problem tricking Tiger. But once inside we must move very, very fast. Remember your targets and stick to them. May the spirits protect you."

"And you," they chorused.

They moved out of the clearing, taking a forest path, every fifth man a Chinese speaker. Luckily for Bolan there was no shortage of them in the force. Many of the Meo in the Triangle were from Yunnan, the province of southern China where most Meo still live.

The rest of the force lined the path to see them off. As Bolan passed, faces smiled, hands touched him, voices whispered encouragement. From commander he had become their hero, the man who had single-handedly saved the train from destruction. His unsmiling modesty only increased their admiration. He was a human hero.

The column descended the ridge and came onto the dirt road leading to the hardsite. Just before the last bend, Bolan was tied across a saddle. He would enter the hardsite as a corpse rather than a prisoner. A white prisoner would attract too much interest.

The gates loomed ahead. As the column neared, a searchlight came on from one of the flanking towers. Its beam swept the column up and down, lingering on the prisoners. A rider broke from the column and galloped up to the gates. He wore a bloodstained uniform with bullet tears and a bloodstained bandage on his head.

"Green frogs," he shouted. "Captain Wong's group

returning." Green frogs was the password. They got that from the prisoners.

"What happened?" asked a voice from a tower.

"Montagnards attacked us," replied the rider. "We beat them but lost Captain Wong and four men."

"Killed?"

"Yes."

"And the wages?" another man asked.

"Safe."

"Open the gates!" the first voice called.

The gates swung open, the searchlight went out, and a smaller arc light came on, forming a spotlight by the entrance. The column filed under the flag-bedecked archway with the Chinese inscriptions. First came horses with the money, then horses with the bodies.

The prisoners appeared. "Look at those necks," said a voice. "The colonel will be pleased. Lots of flesh to test his swords on."

Guffaws greeted the remarks.

As the column entered the parade ground it formed ranks. From his upside-down position Bolan surveyed the lay of the land. The parade ground was in darkness, but beyond it were lots of streetlights and he could hear music.

A door opened from a barrack on the side. An officer and an assistant stepped out and walked briskly to the forming ranks.

"Where is Sergeant Tsepo?" the officer called.

"Here I am, sir," replied the false sergeant.

"What's this about an ambush?" asked the officer.

"We were jumped as we were getting off the train," said the sergeant. "They were waiting for us at Py Fung."

A flashlight shone in the sergeant's face. "You're not Tsepo," said the assistant. The beam swept the column. "Sir, these are not Captain Wong's men."

"Searchlight!"

Night turned into day. But almost immediately muzzles flashed. With a puff of smoke and the tinkle of glass the searchlight went out. A moment of stunned silence followed, then all hell broke loose.

"Attack! Attack!" Bolan shouted into the radio set given to him by the Montagnard who released him. "We're inside!"

From up the ridge a green flare fired. A bugle sounded down the road. The radio blared. "Nark to Phoenix. The cavalry's on its way!"

On the parade ground bedlam reigned. Colored tracers flew in all directions, men yelled, horses galloped in confusion. A tower flashed as an RPG hit its mark. Windows blew, and a barrack exploded in flames.

But the enemy was not sleeping, either. The inside of the parade ground lit up with a myriad of flashes, and Bolan's commando force began to take casualties.

"Arty! Arty!" Bolan shouted into his set above the din. "Open fire on the parade ground! Willie Peter, all four tubes."

The hills boomed, the sky crackled. Mortar bombs rained on the parade ground as fast as the men could load them. They exploded in showers of white phosphorus, setting trees and tents on fire. But the enemy kept shooting.

"Spread your fire!" Bolan shouted into the radio.

The battery widened the lateral angle. The shells began falling farther apart. Soon the entire area was illuminated.

"Perfect! Now give me Hotel Echo."

The white showers gave way to orange flashes as the mortar crews switched to firing high explosive. By the light of the burning trees Bolan could see bodies cartwheel in the air and men fall, sliced by shrapnel.

Two groups of Tiger men were running toward the parade ground carrying machine guns. They dropped to the ground near the tree line and proceeded to set up their guns.

"Number three tube!" Bolan shouted. "Right thirty, down ten!"

The machine gun crews ducked as a bomb from number three mortar exploded near them. A moment later, however, both groups were firing their Browning .50-caliber guns, the famous battlefield broom, hosing the parade ground with 12.7mm slugs.

From the road came the blare of a bugle and the thunder of hooves. Gooseflesh broke out on Bolan's arms. With the big .50s in action, the cavalry was riding to certain doom. It would be carnage.

"Arty, arty, all four tubes lock into number three! Number three down ten. All four go!"

A cluster of bombs warbled overhead. The inside of the tree line lit up with orange explosions. The machine gun positions disintegrated, arms and legs flying through the air.

"Bingo!"

"Ayu!"

A mass of black riders poured through the gates. They fanned out into the hardsite, heading for their assigned targets. Many horses carried two men apiece, miniature gun platforms flying through the night, the rider shooting to the right, the passenger to the left.

A group of riders with pack animals stopped by Bolan. Nark and Stressner were among them. They had brought a spare horse for Bolan with a pepesha attached to the saddle. Bolan mounted, and the group galloped off in the direction of the industrial sector.

Three abreast they thundered down an alley bordered by opium warehouses, the area dark and deserted. But not deserted enough. A squad of Tiger troops appeared, running for the parade ground. The three white riders rose in their saddles, and the perforated barrels of their pepeshas flickered flame. The squad scattered and the riders flew by.

They crossed a square, turned some corners, and the administration building came into view. Muzzles flashed from open windows. But there was no stopping Bolan now. He had neither the time nor the energy to work out some clever, safe way of taking the building. Horses tumbled, men died, but the charge continued.

One of the windows was closed and in darkness. Bolan steered his mount for it. At the last moment, still on the gallop, he jumped to the ground, bounced, and crashed through the window amid flying glass. The rest of the force followed in his wake, into the office, out into the corridor, some going left, others to the right, shooting up everything in sight.

Within minutes the building was secured. The Tiger communication center was theirs. So was the gold and, most important of all, so were Tiger's international files.

IT WAS A VERITABLE ALI BABA'S CAVE. In the files were the names of every Tiger agent and contact around the world. There were names of shippers, importers, distributors, lists of companies that laundered the money, who invested what and where, the numbers of secret bank accounts, names of paid politicians, crooked cops, enforcers, and district managers. A wealth of data.

One filing cabinet contained all the smuggling networks and the methods used to smuggle heroin into the U.S. In Amsterdam the heroin was inserted into the rectums of airline flight attendants. From Marseilles it was imported inside blocks of marble. Hong Kong sent it in cans of litchi nuts. Colombia dropped it offshore in shallow waters.

"We really hit the jackpot," said Bolan.

"About time," said Nark.

"Got 'em!" shouted Stressner.

The room filled with the crackle of the Crypton as Stressner began transmitting material already penciled by Nark. Bolan's and Nark's eyes met, and Bolan gave him a thumbs-up. For both it was a triumphant moment. After all they had been through, the ups and downs, the nerves, the lack of sleep, and in Bolan's case, the severe pain he still carried...finally, the payoff.

Bolan imagined the scene at the other end, the Stony Man Farm radio room triple-staffed for the occasion, April in command, the hustle and bustle as the incoming messages were decoded and passed on to the appropriate offices.

The radio blared, "Colonel, come quick!" It was Vang Ky. "We found the fish. In the refinery."

"They've located the management!" Bolan shouted to Nark and ran out.

He came out of the building, mounted his horse, and galloped through the dark, deserted alleys. There had hardly been any fighting in the industrial sector. It was all taking place in the residential part. Bolan could hear mortar warble overhead as artillery gave support. The sky over the residential section glowed with fires.

The refinery milled with Montagnards wandering between rows of vats steaming with frothy liquids that workmen were stirring. Vang Ky ordered the night shift to carry on for the education of the troops. For most of them, it was their first opportunity to see what happened after they sold their harvest.

One of Vang Ky's assistants led Bolan through the crowd past the steaming vats to the foot of a staircase. It was here that the action was taking place. The steps were littered with bodies of Montagnards shot by Tiger troops occupying the landing above. Now Bolan understood why the main body of the assault force was on R&R. There was no room in the stairway for more than a handful.

"They are on the third floor," Vang Ky reported.

Bolan unslung his submachine gun and climbed the stairs cautiously, followed by Vang Ky and some Montagnards. He came to a corner, took a dead man's beret, and placed it on the muzzle. He stuck the beret around the corner. A bullet sang past, and Bolan withdrew.

"We'll have to try something else," he said.

"I say we burn them," said Vang Ky.

"I want them alive," said Bolan.

A metal object bounced down the stairway. "Grenade!" shouted Vang Ky, and the recon party descended frantically to the ground floor. But it was only a metal cap.

From the landing above, a voice laughed. "Fooled you, eh? Next time it will be for real."

A Montagnard ran up the stairs and let off an angry burst from his AK-47. From the landing an M-16 replied.

"Colonel, what are we going to do?" asked Vang Ky.

"I'm thinking, Major," said Bolan, eyeing the elevator. The car was on the ground floor, the door open. Inside stood a wheelbarrow with a load of brown jelly, raw opium.

"Colonel, we cannot send men in the elevator," said Vang Ky. "They will be killed before they open the gate."

"I wasn't thinking of sending men, Major." Bolan pulled up the aerial on his radio. "Phoenix to Pincus."

"Pincus," replied the copilot of the Ilyushin. A former navy SEAL, Bolan had put him in charge of dynamiting.

"Where are you?"

"Mining the warehouses."

"I got a target and I need some explosive. Send me a couple of kilo. I'm in the refinery."

"Any particular sort?"

"Give me a mixture. And I'll need caps, wire and a bravo mama."

"Coming up."

Bolan told Vang Ky his plan. "The explosive will be here in a few minutes."

"You're a man of imagination, Colonel," said Vang Ky. In the same breath he added, "When can we have our gold?"

Flattery won't get you anywhere, guy, Bolan thought. "When the fighting's over," he replied.

They lit up cigarettes and waited for the dynamite, watching the work around them. From where they stood Bolan could see several processes going on at once. In one section opium was being boiled with water and lime to extract the morphine. In another the morphine was being solidified with ammonia. Farther on, beyond drying and filtering machines, stood rows of vats with thermometers where morphine was being dissolved in acetic anhydride to bond chemically into diacetylmorphine, the chemical name for heroin.

"Very interesting," said Vang Ky, nodding at the activity.

"Yeah," said Bolan. "Deadly, too."

"What happens in the laboratories behind the partition?"

"That's where the heroin's purified and solidified," Bolan replied. "Before you get the final product there are four or five stages through which the crude heroin must go. You must treat the heroin with chloroform, sodium carbonate, charcoal, hydrochloric acid, ether. Then you have something that will destroy the body as surely as viper's venom. But it looks harmless, just a white powder."

"Complicated business," said Vang Ky, sucking his teeth.

A stir by the door told Bolan his goodies had arrived. Two Montagnards appeared carrying sacks. Bolan emptied the contents. The explosive came in bricks that carried such names as Plastite and Nepolit, Pirkinsaure and Ammon Saltpeter, and Sprengmunition 02.

It was old East German stock, some dating from World War II, unloaded as part of fraternal aid to some Communist movement in the Sudan. The movement's leader promptly sold it for some capitalist greenbacks.

Bolan called for the wheelbarrow from the elevator. He emptied it and stacked the bricks inside. He inserted detonator caps and attached firing wire to them. Then he covered the bricks with the raw opium.

A Chinese-speaking Meo who could write found a sheet of paper and wrote "ultimatum" in large Chinese characters. The paper was affixed to a stick, and the stick was stuck into the jelly.

They wheeled the barrow into the cage and positioned it so the wire would not show. Bolan passed the other end through a crack in the floor and out the elevator shaft. He attached that end to a small hand blasting machine, the bravo mama.

The assault unit assembled. A Montagnard called up the stairway to alert Tiger that an ultimatum was being sent. Another Montagnard pressed the second-floor button and closed the gate.

In the stairway, Bolan waited, machine in hand, fingers crossed. Old explosives tended to deteriorate and sometimes failed to go off. That's why he had asked for a mixture.

The cage rose. Bolan heard it come to a stop on the landing above. There was a lot of chatter from the soldiers, then Bolan heard the gate being opened. He twisted the handle on the machine, and an ear-splitting roar shook the building. Bolan dropped the machine, grabbed his gun, and bounded up the stairs.

The landing was strewn with chunks of concrete and twisted girders. The air was full of dust, and flames flickered. On Bolan's left came the sound of running, shouting men. Tiger soldiers were coming to see what had happened. Before they got to the landing, to be engaged by the Montagnards, Bolan had already slipped past.

He climbed to the third floor, colliding with a soldier coming down. The pepesha spat flame at point-blank range, and the man rolled down the stairs. As Bolan emerged onto the landing, he saw muzzles spitting flame from down a corridor. Bolan ducked and backed out. He primed a frag and rolled it down the corridor. A scurry of feet and shouts of alarm were lost in an explosion.

Bolan crossed the landing and entered a large storage area. The floor was full of crates marked with Chinese characters and piles of sacks marked Tiger Brand No. 4, the final product, ninety-nine percent pure heroin, ready for shipment to the States. The place was silent and dark, the only light coming from a distant bulb.

Bolan hesitated, wondering what to do. It was a perfect place to be ambushed. Why not try some psycho-warfare? Liu and company must be hoping for relief, otherwise they would not be making a stand. Why not fulfill their hopes?

Bolan cupped his mouth and called out, "Hey, guys, where are you? It's me, Jack. Jack Fenster. I've brought relief. I'm with the Thais. Where are you?"

He crouched and listened. Perhaps the trick would work. After all, no one but Big Bottom, the mahout, and himself knew what happened to Jack Fenster. And why shouldn't Fenster come back to help his colleagues if he survived the ambush?

Footsteps. Cautious footsteps. A voice called quietly, "Jack?"

Bolan tiptoed in the direction of the sound and went down behind a forklift. Steps approached.

"Jack, where are you?"

A roly-poly individual in a golfing shirt and slacks appeared. In his hand he held a handkerchief with which he constantly wiped his face. To Bolan it was obvious the man felt he was performing a feat of great courage by making the trip in the dark alone. Wrong! He was not alone. Behind him came a Tiger soldier, weapon at the ready. Bolan let them pass.

"Jack?"

Bolan rose and moved like a cat. A knife stabbed the soldier, a hand covered the fat man's mouth. "Jack is in hell," he whispered into the man's ear. "And he wants you to join him."

The man's eyes bulged and he began shaking. The smell of urine filled the air. As his bladder emptied, the shaking subsided.

Bolan pointed the knife at him. "Now, where is everyone? Use your hand."

The man pointed behind him.

"Any soldiers?"

The man shook his head.

Bolan turned him. "Lead the way."

They moved through the gloom past the crates and the stacks of Tiger Brand No. 4, Bolan keeping his ears wide open for any unusual sound. But there was none. The only sound was the muffled gunfire from the floor below as the Montagnards fought it out with Tiger troops.

They came to a partition with a door. An office of some sort. The door was closed, light came through the opaque glass, but no sound emanated from it.

"In there?" Bolan whispered.

The man nodded.

"Go inside and leave the door open behind you," Bolan whispered. "Understood?"

The man nodded.

"Go," said Bolan, releasing him.

The man walked to the door, opened it, and went inside. Through the doorway Bolan could see an office with an Oriental carpet and armchairs in which sat the directors. They watched their colleague enter with fear and expectation. But there was an additional expression on their faces, and it sent blood rushing to Bolan's head. They resembled men left leaderless.

A moment later, as he stepped into the office after roly-poly, Bolan's premonition was confirmed. The directors were there, but Colonel Liu was not among them.

12

From a window up in the refinery Bolan gazed on the scene of destruction.

The Tiger hardsite lay in ruins, the air swirling with smoke. By the light of dawn he could see groups of Montagnards going through the rubble.

In the residential section only the guest villa was left standing; everything else had burned or been blown up.

It was a picture of desolation, but desolation with a menace, for somewhere amid those ruins, Bolan's enemy was hiding.

From the directors, Bolan had learned that Liu had left the conference shortly before the battle broke out. It was the last day of the annual meeting, and they were working late. But Liu's servants said their master never showed up, which would indicate he was en route when the fighting started. What happened to him after that, no one knew. None of the soldiers questioned had seen him. All the other directors had stayed put, scared, unarmed, and pathetically easily taken.

To Bolan there could be only one explanation for Liu's disappearance: he must have decided on the spot that the battle was lost. He would have had good reasons, not the least of which was that when the fighting began the enemy was already inside the camp. And having decided all was lost, what would an opium warlord do, lead his troops in a death-defying stand?

Hardly.

He would escape or hide.

Bolan was sure Liu did not escape. The camp had been surrounded from the start by his Montagnards, no helicopter took off, and no secret tunnels running under the perimeter had been discovered.

But he would find Liu. It was his mission.

He realized it was of no consequence where fate might lead a man. If there was evil there, it must be resisted, struggled against, fought to the end.

A PLACE, ANY PLACE, is only godforsaken if men do nothing—if they do not stand up for what is right. Wherever a man finds himself, all that counts is that he fight for the civilized values he believes in.

To profess principles but not be prepared to back them up is to be without principles.

What matter where you die, what matter if you die—when all that matters is that you fought for the right.

But there are occasions when, as every soldier knows, inaction itself is one's fate. Today Mack Bolan knew better, in his dangerous and deceit-filled new world, the value of discretion, the valor of keeping his distance, of not jumping in before the true root of the atrocity had a chance to reveal itself. As The Executioner, and as Colonel John Phoenix, his heavy fate had become apparent: he must forever hit at the root, the core, of evil itself—go to the very heart of darkness itself, and react sanely to what he found there.

To be sane in a hideously distorted world, shock tilted, ringing with terror, was sanity indeed.

He would face the challenge once again, in his latest return to the ancient hellgrounds of Southeast Asia.

He knew that he was about to confront a revelation of his fate that would challenge his very sanity.

And his response would be inevitable: hit at the heart of the horror, strike the pumping source, even if the writhing heads of the Hydra commit atrocities all around, ignore them at last! Strike only at the heart, dig up the root, hit the final perpetrator.

Mack Samuel Bolan was an old-fashioned warrior, dedicated to his nation and his duty. He took his soldiering seriously. He had no other choice. So to go for the psychic heart every time required tireless energy and a unique skill.

It was in Vietnam that the warrior first honed his skills and found his mission.

As the leader of a deadly penetration team, he ranged at will across the DMZ, teaching Savage Man that any hope of sanctuary in Bolan's kind of everlasting war was a contradiction in terms.

There was only so much that one man could do in Nam, but Bolan did it better and more often. He supremely left his mark upon the enemy and on the land.

In the process, he earned a label that would stick. Sergeant Bolan had become The Executioner, a legendary figure from the Mekong Delta to Hanoi.

There was another side of him, however, and another side to the legend. Even as his marksmanship and cunning built a lethal reputation, other stories circulated through the jungle that told of a different warrior. This warrior risked his life to carry wounded soldiers and civilians through the lines. He liberated captives, often jeopardized his mission to remain behind with stricken comrades.

Among the villagers, the Executioner became known as Sergeant Mercy.

It required a large and special man to carry both names well, and Bolan was equal to the task. He saw no contradiction in his roles; if anything, they were a natural combination, opposite sides of a single coin. Killing the enemy and caring for the innocent were not distinct and separate tasks for Bolan—they were part and parcel of his duty.

An old-fashioned warrior. Having recognized his duty, launched himself upon the long crusade, there could be no turning back.

If his road had developed a new direction, his enemy adopting new and ever more loathsome disguises on the way, Bolan never deviated from his course.

Against the Cong or mafiosi or the Hydra, it was the same crusade.

War everlasting.

And his enemy was the same single enemy, unchanging.

His enemy was the heart of the Hydra, wherein resides pure evil.

In his Asian jungles he had cut a bloody swath through the arteries of that enemy, the ranks of Savage Man, mobs of cannibals who lived for the Hydra. And when his war had shifted to another front, application of the Bolan Effect to an urban combat zone had hugely stunned the Mafia, decimating family after family. Schooled in guerilla warfare, equipped with all the latest lethal hardware, Bolan astounded experts by pulling off a victory against syndicate forces that vastly, absurdly outnumbered him. In his wake, the mighty Mafia was shaken and dispirited, an easy mark for Hal Brognola and his *federales*.

As for Bolan's other global war, the John Phoenix campaign of justice by fire, there was only one word for it: blitzkrieg—lightning war. Mobility and firepower were the methods.

Now Bolan faced dramatic new focus as his life term of Executioner brought him closer and closer to the single hellheart of Savage Man.

Perilous territory, full of horror. At first he would be forced to be a helpless witness to it.

And then he would strike at the heart.

Meanwhile there was no rest, no surcease. All around flowed more arteries of the enemy; on this day Mack

Bolan's enemies were legion. But he had slaughtered thousands since the birthing of his war, and although a dozen more rose to take the place of every fallen savage, he had stood his ground and with grim determination fought against the tide. There was no question that he would prevail.

He had a tactic as powerful as any weapon. This weapon was one of perception and timing, not caliber or trajectory.

Once he had been an outlaw. Now, for a time at least, he was sanctioned in his work. The secret weapon was that Bolan was not a fixed object.

He did not sit like a landmark in one spot, waiting for the natural forces to find him and wear him down.

He would never become a testament to entropy, to the destructive power.

As a new day dawned, Bolan understood profoundly how much he was not like these tropical lands of the Far East, worn and worked on beyond recognition by time and war.

At the window in the refinery, Mack Bolan looked out and meditated on the gray mist rolling off the low surrounding hills, down toward the thicker trees of the flatlands.

Like the mist, he would prevail by adapting his form. He would roll over any obstacle in his path.

Like the mist, no jungle could stop him in his mission.

Mack Bolan would pursue Liu to the very end.

Liu's directors, cowering in fear even before the refinery battle broke out, were now locked in the same office where Bolan had first found them, gathered together without weapons but deep in the mire of their propositions and dirty deals of killing and staying alive: vicious vermin, chewing at each others vitals in the face of death instead of uniting in the face of attack.

They would stay there, under lock and key, until Nark, representing the CIA, blew the place sky high.

Bolan descended to the ground floor where Heath and the copilot were finishing mining the refinery. It was the last installation to be mined on the hardsite.

"Everything is wired up to one bravo mama," said Heath. "That way when we leave, all it'll take is one turn of the handle."

"Have you done the vault yet?" asked Bolan. The door had to be blown. It was locked, and only Liu knew the combination.

"Thought we'd leave that to last," said Heath. "The vault's right next to the file room. Could damage the files."

"Not if we do it properly," said Bolan. "I promised the Meo the gold when the fighting was over. It's over."

They set out for the administration building. It was daylight, a cold, windy morning.

In the cloudy sky, birds of prey circled, waiting for the humans to leave so they could begin their feast.

"Colonel, when are we moving out?" asked Heath.

"Not before tonight," Bolan replied. "Nark says it'll take that long to transmit all the files. Why?"

"I was wondering. One of those helos on the LZ wouldn't take too much to fix. A Texas Ranger. Big enough to carry all of us. We'd save ourselves a walk."

"Try it," said Bolan. "If we can fly out, so much the better. Only put a guard on it when you're through. I wouldn't like Liu to lay his hands on it."

"You still think he's in the camp, sir?" asked the copilot.

"I'm certain of it," said Bolan. He pulled out the aerial on his radio. "Phoenix to Mr. Ly." Ly was leading the search for Liu.

"This is Ly, Colonel."

"Anything to report?" asked Bolan.

"Colonel, I tried to get you, but your radio did not answer," said Ly. "A prisoner told us he saw Liu near the administration building when the fighting started. I think he is mistaken. We searched everywhere, but we found nothing.''

Blood rushed to Bolan's head. ''Mr. Ly, you must try again. I want the whole area turned upside down. The admin building, the power house, the tool sheds, the warehouses. Everything must be searched all over, do you understand?''

''Colonel, we did that. He is not in the area. If he is in the camp as you say, he must be hiding in the other section, but we must wait for the ruins to cool down. It is very hot there.''

''Mr. Ly, I insist. You must search the—''

The thunder of hooves interrupted him. From around a corner a group of Montagnard riders emerged going at full gallop. The first one rode Nark's horse. It was Liu. The pepeshas in their hands flickered as they bore down on the whites.

Bolan dived to the ground to avoid the tracers. A moment later shapes flew past and over him amid a cacophony of hoofbeats and gunfire. A hoof kicked his head, sending stars dancing before his eyes. By the time the stars cleared, the riders had gone.

Bolan ran to the radio lying on the ground. ''Mr. Ly! Mr. Ly! Liu is escaping! Order the gates closed!'' But he was wasting his breath. The fall had broken the radio.

''Looks like someone else had the idea of switching uniforms,'' said Heath. ''Did you notice one of them rode Nark's horse?''

Nark! Bolan raced for the administration building.

A crowd had gathered outside. He pushed his way through, his heart beating wildly at the thought of what he might find in the file room. He ran into the building and crossed the foyer where naked Montagnards were trying on uniforms left by Tiger. He descended the stairs two at a time, ran into the file room, and sighed with relief. Both were alive.

"Did you get him?" asked Nark, dabbing iodine on a gash in Stressner's scalp.

"They got away," said Bolan, panting. He looked at the open vault gleaming with yellow metal. "So that's where they were."

"We didn't even hear them," said Nark. "Our backs were turned and the radio was on."

"To be KO'd with a gold brick," said Stressner. "Who'll ever believe it?"

Bolan inspected the vault. It had a door that could be opened from the inside. The racks were filled with enough gold bars to set up the Montagnards for life.

From the stairway came the sound of feet, and Vang Ky appeared followed by Heath and the copilot. "They took the northern trail," the headman announced. "The gate guards took them for our men," he added by way of an excuse.

"To be expected," said Bolan.

"Must be heading for Burma," said Nark.

Bolan walked to where two backpack radio sets stood against a wall. They were Russian Z-10s, among the communication equipment parachuted the previous night. No one was using them because the small sets were handier, but these had a superior range.

"What are you doing?" asked Nark, seeing Bolan strap one on.

"Going after Liu," said Bolan. "I'll leave you to blow up the place. I'll check in every hour on the hour, wherever you are."

"John, don't be foolish," said Nark, going up to him. "Why risk your life for one man? The mission is over."

"No, Nark," Bolan replied. "Drug syndicates are like hydras. To destroy them you have to cut off *all* their heads. If I'm not at the rendezvous, leave without me. I'll make my way back somehow."

"Colonel, let me come with you," said Heath.

"You fix that chopper," said Bolan. "I may need it yet." He turned to Vang Ky. "Well, Major, the gold is all yours. Our deal is complete." He took off the watch and handed it to him. "Thanks for letting me use it."

"And the other thing?" asked Vang Ky.

"You'll be contacted," Bolan replied. "Should something happen to me, Nark will handle it. He knows. You will provide security until Nark is through?"

"You have my word."

"Sombaj, Major. See you guys."

He ran upstairs, picked up a Kalashnikov, and rode off. A quarter of an hour later he was galloping on the northern trail toward Burma, determined not to leave Southeast Asia until he had settled scores with Liu. He owed it to Janet.

Janet Wynn, dead at twenty-two.

A bright girl. A nice girl. In her second year of medical school at the University of Miami she met Bob, a handsome intern. He invited her to a party where, halfway through, people began "chasing the dragon," as heroin smoking is called.

When Bob offered Janet some she refused, but they were such good talkers, he and his friends. Try it, they said, it expands consciousness, it gives new perception, leads to self-discovery. Peer pressure made her give in.

A week later Bob invited her again, and again she smoked.

Like most people, Janet found it a pleasant experience. There were no needles, it did not cost anything, and it gave a nice high. After a smoke she had a feeling of well-being, a warm glow, and she felt part of the crowd.

What Janet did not realize was that she was being set up as an addict so Bob could have another customer, which is how addiction spreads; the addict turns pusher to pay for his habit. There is even a name for such parties; a monkey bait party.

By her tenth party Janet had become an addict, which is when nice Bob turned not-so-nice and told her from now on she would have to pay for her heroin at seventy-five dollars a fix, the standard Tiger price. Bob was a Tiger man.

To raise cash Janet began selling or pawning everything she could. She also switched to the needle to get the maximum out of her purchases, smoking being wasteful. The maximum effect, in turn, increased her dependence on the drug.

Eventually she ran out of money and began stealing from her parents. Her mother caught her and talked to her brother, Rafael Encizo, a member of Bolan's Phoenix Force. He asked Bolan to speak to his niece. Bolan was known to have a way with young people.

The meeting was held in a park, a neutral ground where there was less chance of being overheard. It was akin to a forced date, Bolan going at Rafael's insistence, Janet at her mother's. They were alone, just the two of them, no relatives, no parents.

To Janet's surprise, Bolan was not a stuffed shirt.

If God Almighty ever invented anything better than heroin, he kept it to himself, said Janet.

Bolan said he could understand that.

And the memory of heroin's pleasures! It overpowers the memory of the suffering that accompanied it, said Janet.

Bolan did not contradict her.

Janet could not get over it. She had expected a lecture and instead got understanding; she expected condemnation but got sympathy. Not only that, he was so knowledgeable and actually willing to discuss heroin. At home, she had but to mention heroin and her parents flew into a rage.

Toward the end of their walk she asked Bolan if he had ever taken drugs. He replied no and she asked why

"For one thing, I can't afford them," he said with a self-deprecating smile. "And then," he added, looking into her eyes, "they sort of cut you off from life, don't they?"

Two days later she called him to ask if he knew a way of kicking the habit. He spoke to a doctor who recommended a methadone program. On the first day Bolan accompanied her to the clinic.

In the program with her were a number of former addicts. They formed a group that met once a week at someone's home the way AA people do, a social gathering to keep one another company and give encouragement. Every week it was held in someone else's home. Coffee and cake were served.

One day, however, in addition to coffee the host brought out heroin. He was no patient but a pusher masquerading as one in order to gain the confidence of former addicts with the object of getting them back on the drug. As the smell of heroin filtered through the room, one by one they succumbed.

Janet disappeared from her home, and her mother asked Bolan to find her. He looked for her for a month, eventually finding her in New York City. At first he did not recognize her. An attractive, healthy young woman had become a walking zombie. She was now a full-fledged junkie, mainlining four times a day and peddling the stuff herself to pay for her fix.

It was then that Bolan learned that ninety percent of heroin addicts suffer relapses because the pushers pursue them relentlessly. It was then, too, that he realized fighting dope in the streets with police and courts was a waste of time. One had to strike at the source, go for the head, keep drugs from entering the country.

Bolan asked Janet to help him penetrate Tiger, and she said she would think about it. She was torn between her loyalty to her fellow junkies and her affection for Bolan. Before she could decide, however, Tiger struck.

The ring was taking no chances. One morning, Janet was found dead of a supposed overdose. An autopsy showed her heroin had been cut with rat poison.

That was when Bolan vowed to kill the head of Tiger.

13

The rider in black galloped in relentless pursuit of his enemy. It was late afternoon, and man and beast glistened with sweat. They had been on the go all day, winding their way through steamy jungles, climbing and descending hills, fording streams, and galloping on flat stretches to make up for time lost in picking up tracks on the other side of those streams.

Now he was once more on a flat stretch, galloping on a trail through a forest of sandalwood, eyes watering from the rush of air, face flushed from the heat, deaf to all sound but the rhythmic drumming of hooves as they carried him closer to his prey, his mind concentrating on what he would do to Janet's killer.

And that's what cost him, concentrating on the future instead of the present.

Too late did he realize that the birds no longer sang in the treetops. In the jungle this was a sure sign of an ambush, because while birds will sing when men go by, they clam up when the men stop. By the time he realized this and reined his mount, he was already in the ambush zone. Fate decreed that he undergo capture.

Ahead, a barrier of lianas blocked the trail. To the sides the undergrowth was too thick to pass. When he wheeled his mount to attempt a retreat he found himself staring into the muzzles of pepeshas held by Liu's Montagnard-suited soldiers.

They made him dismount and disarm. He complied; he had no choice. Then they tied him with lianas, one vine around his wrists, another around his neck. He was put back on his horse and they rode off, the soldiers laughing, enjoying their success, the prisoner acutely aware that he was allowing fate the upper hand.

Of all people to get caught like this, he told himself angrily. He who was always lecturing men under his command to concentrate on the task at hand and not to let their minds wander. *If you must think of any moment but the present,* he would tell them, *pause in what you are doing.*

It was little consolation to him that he had been five nights without sleep and that when a mind is tired it begins to wander. A commander was not supposed to let himself be carried away by a mission to the point where his faculties were impaired. Back at the refinery he had already had warning signs that he was overstretching himself when he hesitated on the third floor wondering what to do. Hesitation! The product of a sluggish mind deprived of sleep. But he chose to ignore the warning and play at being superman. Pride, the downfall of men. Fate was trying to tell him something.

A slap in the face from a branch brought his self-critique to an end. They had gone off the trail and were crossing a dense forest. Low hanging branches, pushed aside by the rider ahead, snapped back into his face, delivering powerful stings. The only thing he could do, since his hands were tied at his back, was try to duck in time.

They came to another trail and set off at a trot. They crossed some swampland and after about a half hour's ride entered a rubber plantation. They trotted past rows of palm trees with small cups attached to their trunks for the collection of the latex.

A mansion came into view, a magnificent white building with turrets, a relic from days when Burma was part of the British Empire. The architecture recalled the Taj Mahal. It was set in a park with fountains and beds of exotic flowers. A real palace.

The commander of the party dismounted and ran inside carrying Bolan's gear. While they waited for him on their mounts, a young woman appeared on the first-floor balcony. One look at her told Bolan she was Liu's daughter; the resemblance was striking. Their eyes met, and Bolan inclined his head. He did it unconsciously; she was that kind of a woman. She replied with a bow of her own, an expression of sympathy in her sad eyes. Why was she sad? Bolan wondered.

The officer returned and they rode off. They came to a work area, a large yard bordered by sheds with roofs but no walls. Bolan could see men pouring latex into huge tanks, and there was the smell of formic acid in the air, the acid used to solidify the rubber for shipment.

Beyond the work area were more sheds, these with walls. Bolan was led into one of them. The place stank to high heaven, being a storage shed for solid rubber blocks. In a space in the center was a post supporting the roof. One of the soldiers brought a chain, and they chained Bolan to the post like a dog.

The door closed behind them, plunging the shed into gloom. The only light came through cracks in the walls and roof. Bolan lowered himself to the beaten earth floor and propped his back against the pole. So this was Liu's hideaway.

On the last radio check Nark told him he had found out from a prisoner that Liu had a hideaway in Burma. Nark was looking for maps in the administration building that would give the coordinates.

Hopefully, Nark would find them. Hopefully, too, when he did not hear from Bolan on the next radio check he would put two and two together. And hopefully he would pay the plantation a visit.

An outside rescue was about the only way Bolan could see of getting out. After the caper he pulled the night he was tortured, he doubted Liu would leave much to chance. The chains he had on were a good example.

He was bound solid: cuffs around his wrists, cuffs around his ankles, a chain linking the two with the pole, everything joined by a padlock. No way out of that.

He stretched himself out on the ground, figuring he should rest while he had the chance. Through the cracks in the roof he watched night fall. Bolan began imagining food; he had not eaten since noon of the previous day. Bit by bit his eyelids grew heavy. What was his fate going to reveal to him?

THE STING OF A WHIP on his cheek brought him out of a dream. The light was on, he could feel blood oozing down the side of his face, and he could see a pair of highly polished riding boots. Before he could remember where he was, the whip lashed out a second time, catching him in the neck.

"Get up!" a voice barked.

It was Liu, dressed in a golf shirt and breeches, standing with his feet apart and a long whip in his hand in the pose of a circus animal trainer. And his eyes glared with anger.

But so did Bolan's. He sprang to his feet and charged his tormentor. The other stepped deftly aside, and Bolan was pulled back cruelly by the chain.

The whip flew at Bolan, catching him in the mouth and filling it with blood. "Get up!"

Once more Bolan went for him, and once more Liu stepped aside. But this time the whip moved constantly, forming red welts on Bolan's body, tearing strips from his shirt and trousers, the cracks of the whip mixing with the rattling of the chain as Bolan rolled on the ground to avoid the painful blows.

Finally the whipping stopped. "Better get it into your head, Colonel Phoenix, that here it is I who command. You might be commander at Stony Man Farm, but here you're just another white dog. A white dog, do you understand? Get up!"

Spitting blood, Bolan rose to his feet.

"That's better," said Liu. He wound the whip and went to take a seat on a rubber block. He leaned back in a relaxed manner against the blocks as if on a couch. "And so finally we meet, Stony Man One," he said, crossing his legs. "Don't look so surprised. You're not the only one with an intelligence service, though I must admit mine leaves a lot to be desired of late. You'll be pleased to hear that the man who interrogated you has had his head cut off. So has the man who interrogated Nark. They actually fell for that cock-and-bull story you fed them about a Russian-sponsored Montagnard uprising." He recrossed his legs. "I need some answers. What happened to my directors?"

"They're dead," said Bolan.

"You killed them?"

"Yes."

"Why?"

"It is part of the war against the drug rings," said Bolan. "The ringleaders will be executed."

"Is that why you were following me? To kill me as well?"

"Yes."

"You're a real St. George, aren't you?"

Bolan said nothing, observing his enemy in silence. Close up Liu looked even more the prince of darkness than when Bolan saw him the first time through field glasses, the day he and Nark reconnoitered the Tiger hardsite. Now, in addition to the handsome, satanic face and the muscular build, Bolan was conscious of Liu's charisma. He was also conscious of Liu's superior intelligence. A formidable enemy.

"When you killed my directors did you just bump them off or did you give them a speech first?" asked Liu.

"I read them the charge," Bolan lied.

"Which was?"

"Crimes against humanity."

"How American," Liu mused. "You people are so moral...when it suits you. Did you know that in 1900 during the Boxer Rebellion when China was fighting to rid itself of the opium trade imposed on it by the Europeans, the U.S. sided with the Europeans? Righteous Americans like yourself went around slaughtering Chinese in the name of free trade. Today they are equally righteous about preventing free trade. How do you square that, Colonel Phoenix?"

Bolan said nothing. History was full of whores.

"The question is too profound for you, is it?" asked Liu, contempt in his voice. He stared at Bolan for a while as if studying him. "I understand you are an adept of *kenjutsu*."

"I have studied *kenjutsu*, yes," Bolan replied.

"The reason I ask is that tomorrow we are holding our annual *tameshigiri*. I will be trying out swords on the necks of some criminals, and I propose to add yours to them. Since you are a swordsman, I will give the opportunity to die sword in hand. Unless you would prefer the block."

"Sword in hand will be fine," said Bolan.

Again Liu stared at Bolan as if studying him. Abruptly, he rose. "Very well, my adjutant will come for you in the morning so you can wash and dress. Sleep well."

Bolan watched him walk out.

A little later the door opened and two soldiers entered. One carried a bucket, the other a tray of food. They undid Bolan's hands and left him to eat.

The gladiator submits, thought Bolan. Not that he had any complaints; he was starving and the food was excellent. There was noodle soup, a shrimp dish, vegetables and rice, *ngapi* sauce—a Burmese specialty—mangoes, and Mandalay beer.

When he finished he called to the guards for a light for a cigarette. He pondered the passivity that commanded his actions, that cast a pall over his soul so deep that the flash of fate's vision would soon be inescapable in the darkness. What was he about to endure, about to see?

When he finished his cigarette, Bolan sat in the dark, his mind on the fight to come.

He must not be afraid, he told himself.

Fear was the greatest obstacle to concentration.

Then, too, it was selfish to worry about losing your life. He had been put on this earth to promote the good of man, not his own welfare.

Get beyond love and grief: exist for the good of man.

One of the Four Oaths of Bushido, the way of the warrior.

From some recess of his memory Bolan recalled the words of Sensei Matsubara, his *kenjutsu* master, on the side of a mountain in Virginia: *The way of the warrior is the resolute acceptance of death.*

This means choosing death whenever there is a choice between life and death.

If you can accustom yourself to the idea of death you become one with the way of the warrior.

You can pass through life with no possibility of failure and perform your office properly.

The way is not technique.

The way is the right spirit.

God, give me the right spirit, Bolan prayed.

THE SWORD WAS A BLUR, and the Yao bandit toppled, brains spilling from his severed skull.

Bolan, a spectator, bowed his head and the crowd applauded.

It was the fourteenth death of the morning and they had all been grisly, the main object of the executions being not so much to kill the man as to test the sword.

For this purpose various cutting techniques were used. They ranged from the simple across-the-waist-in-two, to the more sophisticated shoulder-to-opposite-nipple. The last one had been horizontally-above-the eyes.

Every technique required a special pose. The victims were made to lie sideways on blocks, hung from bars, were spread-eagled between bamboo poles or simply held by guards in a particular position.

The end result of these elaborate cuts and poses was that death was seldom instantaneous. To Bolan this was the worst example of Animal Man in his life to date. He did not fully realize it yet but the event was to be an inescapable exorcism for him.

About a hundred people were watching the executions, mainly Tiger soldiers with a few Burmese plantation workers. The mood was as festive as if it were a bullfight. The fact that men and not animals were being killed bothered no one but Bolan.

In Burma, as in Thailand, Montagnards were a slave class, considered no better than animals. Not even in death was any respect shown them. The bodies were not disposed of until they had been hacked some more to test other swords.

The grim business took place in a sandy enclosure red with blood. To the side were tables where the results were noted. After each execution the sword was brought to Liu who examined how the blade cut through bone, how the fat stuck to the blade and how the iron was discolored.

A scribe committed Liu's comments to paper. The observations would be included in the certificate that went with the sword as well as inscribed on the tang, the part of the blade that went inside the hilt.

Bolan watched the proceedings from the front row of the spectator benches. He was dressed in a white *gi*, a black *hakama*—a divided skirt of the kind samurais wore—and raffia sandals. In his lap lay a beautiful sword. He prepared to execute Liu with it.

Earlier that morning the adjutant, who was sitting next to him, took him to the mansion to show him Liu's private collection of swords. Bolan was told he could have any weapon he wanted. He chose a sixteenth-century *katana*, a samurai long sword.

The Japanese weapon was one any sword collector would have given his eyeteeth for. The scabbard was of finely lacquered wood, colored cherry red, overlaid with a silver mesh. The hilt was of ray skin bound in leather thongs with silver pommels decorated with chrysanthemum designs. The guard was of bronze and silver.

As for the blade, it was of Osufane steel, hand tempered. A clover flower pattern of burl grain ran along the tempered line, the hallmark of a famous swordmaker of the time. The blade was as sharp as a razor and had not a trace of discoloration. Bolan could not have asked for a better weapon.

It surprised him little that Liu would throw open his private collection to him. A man whips a man then makes a grand gesture. It was to be expected of an individual who saw himself as a god. From the adjutant Bolan learned that Liu's title in Chinese was Lord of Life and Death. This place of ritual had locked Bolan into a myth and a struggle older than man.

"How many more executions?" Bolan asked. The Yao's body was being dragged out of the enclosure by a pony. The corpse was hacked beyond recognition.

"One more man," replied the adjutant.

Only it was not a man. The next victim was a boy. To Bolan he looked no more than fourteen. Tears flowed down the boy's face, and he was shaking with terror. His wrists were tied at the front, and he had a cord around his neck, the usual way prisoners were led in.

"You execute children, too?"

"He stole a chicken," said the adjutant. They spoke English.

"And for that you're going to kill him?"

The adjutant shrugged. "The colonel ordered."

A blindfold was tied around the boy's head. His wrists were undone so he could hold his hands over his head, the pose for the next cut. The cord from his wrists was used to tie his ankles so he would not run away. A name was called out, and a young soldier rose from the spectator benches. He was not much more than sixteen.

"A cadet," said the adjutant.

The cadet went up to Liu who handed him a sword. He bowed to Liu, then to the audience, then stationed himself at the boy's side. The boy continued shaking, his hands held high in a position of surrender.

"Ichi no do," Liu ordered loudly.

"Across the chest," explained the adjutant.

The cadet raised his sword and swung at the boy. A red gash appeared on the boy's chest and he fell backward screaming. As he rolled in the sand in agony, the blindfold came off. The cadet gazed at him, a stupid expression on his face.

Liu shouted something, and the cadet moved in on the boy, sword raised. Now there followed a macabre game of cat and mouse, the cadet slashing, the boy rolling to avoid the blows, sand flying, the boy screaming, the crowd on its feet yelling with delight.

Bolan bent his head to avoid the spectacle. On the way to the enclosure the adjutant had told him that if he so much as tried to disrupt the proceedings the colonel had ordered that a hundred Montagnards be executed.

"Tsuki!" shouted Liu. Thrust.

A high-pitched scream rent the air as the blade pierced the boy's heart. The crowd applauded as the cadet ran to Liu with the sword dripping blood. The colonel took one look at it and threw it down with disgust. He shouted orders and left the enclosure.

There was a stir in the crowd and faces turned to Bolan. The long nose was next. The enclosure was cleared of tables and equipment. Soldiers appeared with buckets of sand and rakes, and the bloodstains were covered over. In minutes the ring was ready for the main event.

Bolan stared at the ground between his feet in silent communion with his Creator. *God, give me the right spirit.*

A short while later Liu returned. He no longer wore a uniform but was dressed like Bolan in a white *gi* and a black *hakama*. In his hand he held a samurai's *katana* similar to Bolan's except that instead of lacquered wood, his scabbard was of gold encrusted with lapis lazuli.

Liu entered the enclosure and faced Bolan. With a gesture of the head he bid him enter. Bolan rose and entered the ring. For a while the two men faced each other in silence, Liu looking at Bolan as if he were studying him. Then Liu drew his sword. Bolan followed. Both threw their empty scabbards in the sand.

Holding the swords with two hands in front of them at an angle of forty-five degrees, the men faced each other, standing stock-still. Both had their eyes on the line from the tips of their weapons to the opponent's throat. Both were projecting their life forces, their *ki*, as it is called in the East.

It was an exercise that required tremendous concentration, possible only if the mind was completely empty. The slightest thought would detract from the *ki* pressure. Feeling the slack the other would take advantage and move in. It was an exercise in willpower as much as physics.

The long swords gleamed in the sunlight. The crowd was completely silent. Seconds turned to minutes, the sun beat down, the heat grew, the tension became unbearable. For how long could they keep it up?

"Eee-yiii!" Liu charged, his feet raising sand, his sword going up for a sky-to-earth cut.

Bolan watched him come without moving a muscle.

He stood completely unprotected. In a moment the impending blow would cleave him in two. The fight was practically over. Liu was going to kill Bolan with his first blow.

Then something happened that brought a gasp from the crowd. As Liu's sword began its descent, Bolan stepped sideways. By then Liu's attack was fully committed with no possibility of his changing the angle of the cut. The sword swished through thin air.

A murmur ran through the crowd. Who was this man? The way Bolan had reacted was the act of a swordsman who fought in the spirit of *munen muso*: no conception, no design. The phrase meant the ability to act calmly and naturally even in the face of danger. It was the highest accord with existence, when a man's words and actions were spontaneously the same. Rare indeed were the men capable of it.

Bolan's horror at the executions, which had appalled his imprisoned eyes, turned to pure power as their avenging became his task.

Now that they had gone into motion, Bolan and Liu continued to move, circling each other, Liu changing his stance to a *hasso*, his sword raised above his head to the right. Bolan continued with his sword in the *jodan* position, held straight out at a forty-five-degree angle.

To the spectators the change in Liu's position indicated he intended to end the contest. The death of the long nose would not be preceded by a display of sword fighting. The Lord of Life and Death was going for a quick kill.

Step by step they walked the thousand-mile road, Bolan keeping Liu company every inch of the way, moving sideways, backward, forward, his *ki* always flowing, his whole being concentrating on the task at hand, his mind empty of thought.

The righteousness of Bolan's cause, the readiness to accept death in the cause of mankind, gave him tremendous powers of concentration. No thought entered his mind because there was nothing to worry about. There was only one way on this earth for him and he was on it: do good for mankind and fight evil.

But Liu was worrying.

The unsuccessful charge had rattled him. It was like charging a phantom. Liu asked himself if the American was one of those who could sense an attack in advance. It was said that some men could do this. They were able to register the intent, that spurt of radiant energy emitted a moment before it is converted into action.

If so, Liu knew he was in trouble. Instead of killing the American, the American might kill him. Unlike Bolan, Liu had not entered the fight to die; he had entered the fight to win. The thought that he might not win forced him to consider a number of techniques to kill Bolan quickly.

"Eee-yiii!"

Liu's charge was premature. Everyone could see it. Just what made him do it no one could tell, not even Bolan. Liu may have realized he was losing his *ki* and decided to move before Bolan could take advantage. Or perhaps with his concentration wavering he was unable to feel Bolan's *ki* any longer—you cannot feel the other man's *ki* if yours is not out—and he mistakenly thought it was time to move in.

Either way, Liu thought, and that was what cost him his life. In *kenjutsu* one had to feel a move.

Once more Bolan watched Liu come. Once again he waited until Liu's attack was committed before moving out, and this time as Liu passed him he brought his sword down on Liu's neck. A red gash appeared in the pale flesh. Liu's legs buckled and he fell to his knees, rocking, blood spurting from his neck.

Bolan stepped back and raised his sword.

The crowd rose to its feet.

The sword in Bolan's hand flew down, and in a silent

ending to the day's butchery, the Lord of Life and Death, heroin king of Asia, was executed.

The exorcism was over. The most hideous experience of his incarnation as Colonel Phoenix was over for Mack Bolan.

He had been trapped in a purposeless knot, the struggle between life and death, when the real struggle, the war between good and evil, had been put aside by the maddening and miasmic pull of the Far East, a murderous place on a bad day....

He was purged now, and he would never allow such executions again. He had submitted to the ritual of death long enough. Now he prepared to face the future alone, to fight the good fight by fighting for the good, free of the corruption of others, of ancient societies and modern agencies.

Oh God, give me April, and home.

14

In a flash Bolan was out of the ring and running, the crowd on his heels. It was an undignified exit, but this was no time to stand on ceremony. All the right spirit in the world will not stop a bullet, and many in the audience were armed.

Bolan headed for the mansion. It was his only hope. In the mansion were his clothes as well as his radio and gun. Without them he was lost. He knew where gun and radio were, having spotted them that morning.

He streaked through the palms, sword in hand, outdistancing his pursuers. The fear of a man pursued by a mob ready to tear him apart lent him wings. In their eyes Bolan had read the righteous rage of men deprived of a livelihood. By killing Liu he had put an end to Tiger Enterprises, and a lot of people would be out of work.

Paradoxically, it was the mob's hate that probably saved him. So intent were they on catching him alive, to make him suffer, that no one thought of shooting at him.

He ran into the mansion through the front entrance, sword ready to slash his way through. But the house was empty, as the guards and servants had been at the executions. He bounded up the main staircase.

On the second landing he turned into a corridor and ran past the changing room to the room with the radio and gun. The door was locked! He lunged at it, but it was useless. There was not enough space in the corridor to give him momentum. He tried kicking it down, but he only hurt his foot. A boot might have done it, but not a raffia sandal.

From the staircase came shouting as the mob poured into the house.

"This way!" said a woman's voice.

Bolan spun around. In an open doorway stood Liu's daughter. He ran inside, and she closed the door after him. It was a study full of medical books. She pulled him through it into a bedroom and opened a closet.

"In here!"

The door shut, plunging him into darkness. The only light came from the keyhole, and he noticed that there was no key. He crouched among clothes scented with her perfume, listening at the keyhole.

From the corridor came the sound of boots. Doors banged.

A knuckle rapped on the front door of her apartment, boots crossed the floor of the study, and a man's voice spoke apologetically. The monologue lasted for a minute, the boots retreated, the front door closed.

Bolan waited for word from her. But there was no sound. Had she left too? Then he heard it, a muffled sob.

Bolan emerged from the closet. She was sitting by the dresser, sobbing into her hands.

Bolan's insides tightened. Liu was evil, he had to die, but none of that changed the fact that a daughter had lost a father.

Bolan went up to her.

He stood in silence.

"I am sorry, but it had to be done," he said after a while.

She nodded and went on weeping quietly. He remained by her side, immobile, in a gesture of sympathy. In the corridor the sound of slamming doors receded.

Suddenly there was another rap on the front door.

Bolan moved back into the closet and again crouched by the keyhole, this time looking through.

A man in the uniform of a captain entered the bedroom. Bolan recognized him from the executions. The captain had killed a Montagnard by splitting him in two with one stroke, one of the few clean kills of the day.

"Ty Ling," the captain said. But she paid no attention.

The captain proceeded to speak. Bolan guessed he was presenting his condolences. When he finished he went up and put a hand on her shoulder.

Liu's daughter jumped and backed away, eyes flashing.

The captain resumed speaking. The tone was conciliatory. He held out his arms and moved toward her. She grabbed a candlestick and raised it threateningly. The man shrugged and left the room.

As the front door closed, she put the candlestick down and went into the study. Bolan heard the key turn in the front door lock. She returned and opened the closet.

"You can come out," she said. "They think you ran through the house. You are safe."

"Where is your bathroom?" he asked.

She indicated the door and he went inside. He washed his sword and dried it. When he came out she was standing by the window.

"Put it in the closet," she told him.

He put the sword away and turned to face her. "Why are you doing this?"

"I need your help," she replied, staring out. "I thought if I helped you, you might take me with you. I must get away from here."

"Why must you get away?" asked Bolan.

"So I can marry the man I love," she replied, still staring. "I am a doctor. Until a month ago I was working in a hospital in Mandalay. I met a man there, a German doctor. He was on an exchange. We fell in love, and he asked me to marry him. I came here to ask my father permission to marry. My father refused, told me I had to marry a Chinese, told me he had promised me in marriage to an officer, Weng Shi. He is the second man who came here. Now that my father is dead, Weng Shi will force me to marry him. You are my last chance."

"Are you a prisoner here?" asked Bolan.

She nodded. "The guards have orders not to allow me off the plantation. My father even refused to let me return to the hospital. He was afraid I would elope. When Gunther came here looking for me, my father told him I had left for America, that I had changed my mind." She paused to look at Bolan in a way that reminded him of Liu, that scrutinizing look. "Have you ever been in love?"

"Yes, I've been in love," said Bolan. "Where is it that you want to go, Mandalay?"

"Bangkok," she replied. "Or Rangoon. Gunther is back in Germany. I will take the first plane out. But you don't have to take me that far. I can take a train. I will not burden you, I promise. I am in good health and I can walk far. I can ride, too. I might even be useful to you. I know the trails around here."

"There's only one problem," said Bolan. "I'm not fleeing from marriage, but from people who want to skin me alive. If someone should try to stop me I'll shoot, no matter how many there are. And they'll shoot back. By coming with me you risk being killed."

"I'd rather be dead than spend the rest of my life with Weng Shi. I don't want him and I don't want this life. Hate, kill, hate, kill—that's all they know around here."

"So I've noticed."

"My father started it," she said with a sigh. "In the beginning it was a way of keeping them together, preventing the Ninety-third from disintegrating. The world was against them. To survive they had to hate back. Eventually it got into their blood; like a drug, they needed it to keep going. Ironic, isn't it? While poisoning the world with one drug they became addicts of another.'' She turned to took at Bolan. "If you wish I will pay you. I have money in Bangkok."

"That won't be necessary," said Bolan.

"You will take me?"

"I'll take you, yes. And now let's sit down and figure out how we're going to do it."

IN DARKENED SILENCE Bolan tiptoed down the corridor. Somewhere a clock chimed nine. Otherwise the house was still, everyone at the wake for Liu. The mistress of the house had made a special point of asking that everyone be in the pagoda at nine o'clock that evening for a special prayer: workers, servants, and soldiers united in a joint tribute to the memory of their master. The service was to last an hour... which was exactly how long Bolan had to organize their escape.

He came to a door and opened it with a key Ty Ling had obtained for him. He turned on a flashlight and swept the inside with its beam, half prepared to see his gun and radio gone. But the AK-74 still hung from the coatrack along with the gun belt, and the radio was on the floor by a water cooler.

Bolan collected the gear and went to another door. He opened it with a second key and went to a cupboard. The Montagnard suit hung where he had left it. Below were his boots. He changed back into his clothes, and when he emerged into the corridor a few minutes later, the sixteenth-century samurai was once again the twentieth-century warrior, the Kalashnikov in one hand, the silenced Makarov in the other, the radio on his back.

He left the corridor and tiptoed down the staircase.

From the front steps of the house came the murmur of voices. Guards! So *not* everyone was at the wake for the master. This did not surprise him. Bolan could not see an experienced commander like Weng Shi leaving the house unguarded when the long nose was still free, no matter how much Ty Ling insisted that every member of the plantation be at the service.

Luckily Bolan had planned for this. In the afternoon Ty Ling had drawn him a map of the house, so he knew the layout. When he reached the bottom of the staircase he simply retreated into the house until he got to the main sitting room. He crossed it and climbed out a window. For a minute he crouched in the shadows, listening. Judging that the coast was clear, he sprinted into the trees.

He made his way through the trees to the park and set out along the path, heading for the work yard, his ultimate goal the stables. To walk on the path was risky—he might run into guards—but it would be even more risky to walk off it. The ground was dry, twigs snapped easily, and anyone walking on the path would hear him. This way he had an equal chance, better in fact, for guards usually talked.

The work yard appeared. He crossed it, keeping to the shadow of the buildings. Suddenly he smelled cigarette smoke. He crouched and listened. From around a shed came the murmur of voices. A man coughed. Guards. Bolan slung the Kalashnikov over his back so he could use both hands.

He made his way to the end of the shed and peered. Ahead two cigarette ends glowed in the dark. Bolan worked his way closer, invisible in the shadows. The two guards were also invisible, but after each man took a couple of drags Bolan knew where to shoot. Just as he raised his gun, however, the glows began moving and the men's voices rose.

Bolan lowered the pistol and waited for the argument

to finish. But the soldiers went on arguing, moving all the time. Seconds ticked by, and Bolan did not have seconds to spare. Somehow he had to get them out of the shadows. Then an idea occurred to him. He slipped the magazine clip out of the pistol and extracted a round.

The side of a shed clanged, and the glowing cigarettes stopped their ballet and fell to the ground. Weapons at the ready, the two guards emerged from the darkness. The Makarov hissed twice, and the soldiers crumpled. Bolan ran to make sure they were dead, then pulled the corpses back into the shadows. One man had a couple of offensive grenades attached to his belt, and Bolan took those. For a getaway at night, such goodies were very useful. They were much louder than defensive grenades.

On the other side of the work yard were the stables. Bolan entered the first barn and shone his flashlight. He selected two horses, made friends by feeding them sugar cubes given him by Ty Ling for the purpose, and saddled them. On a hook by the saddles hung a holster for a rifle, and Bolan strapped it on. He attached one horse to the other and led them out, closing the door behind him.

The moon shone peacefully in the sky. The night was still. Bolan mounted, and rider and animals disappeared into the trees. Now began the most nerve-racking part of the adventure: a mile-long trip along a footpath made at walking pace. But there was no other way. A gallop, even a trot, would alert the guards by the house. At night sounds carried far.

It took nearly a half hour to reach the pagoda. It stood in a clearing bordered by palms, a solitary building with a curled-up roof. The windows flickered with light, and from inside came chanting. Bolan observed it from the tree line to see if there were any guards. But there were none. Ty Ling had done her job. She had promised to have everyone inside praying, including the guards. Bolan dismounted, tied the horses, and ran for the entrance.

The inside of the pagoda was packed with humanity, the men on one side, women on the other. On a dais, under a statue of a peak-headed Buddha, lay a coffin draped in the flag of Nationalist China. It was surrounded by candles and flowers, paper money hung from rafters, and the air was heavy with incense.

"Maiouk!" Bolan shouted, stepping inside.

A woman screamed, faces turned, the chanting stopped.

"Anyone speak English?" he called out.

By the coffin, Ty Ling rose to her feet. "What is it you want?"

"Step this way, lady," Bolan commanded. "And tell the people if anyone moves, I shoot. I don't care how many I kill."

Ty Ling addressed the congregation in Chinese, urging calm, then moved toward the entrance through the aisle separating the men and women. Bolan panned the crowd nervously with the Kalashnikov as if he were slightly mad. It was a trick he had learned way back. No professional soldier will try anything with a madman, because you cannot judge his reaction.

Ty Ling came up. "Outside," Bolan ordered.

Ty Ling went out, and Bolan continued waving the gun back and forth. By the coffin he could see Weng Shi look at him, a puzzled expression on his face. Did he smell a rat, Bolan wondered. Was he trying to figure out how Bolan got the key to the room with his gun?

Sixteen...seventeen...eighteen. Bolan counted the seconds, giving Ty Ling time to reach the horses. "Outside" was a code word they had agreed on. It meant everything was going as planned, the horses would be by the path.

Twenty-five, Bolan counted. Ty Ling must be there. He stepped out and ran to join her. Halfway there, a gun opened up and colored tracers flew by. He spun, dropped to one knee, and sprayed the entrance. Figures fell, figures retreated, and he was back running.

He ran into the woods. Ty Ling was already on her horse, holding the reins of his mount. "Go!" he shouted and swung into the saddle as shooting broke out anew. Ty Ling spurred her mount and they galloped off, the shouting and shooting receding in the thunder of hooves and panting of horses.

They crashed through the undergrowth, keeping their heads down to avoid branches. He followed her easily, and soon they came out onto a plain and picked up speed. Now they could really fly. The terrain was flat and solid. But they were also more visible, and the mounted Tiger patrol that emerged from the tree line on the left, attracted by the gunfire, headed straight for them.

"Go right!" Bolan shouted.

"Too long!" Ty Ling shouted back.

Great! he thought. To avoid taking a longer way they were going to get themselves captured. No way could they get past that patrol...unless. Bolan dug his heels into the horse's flanks and veered to meet the patrol. He holstered the Kalashnikov and armed the offensive grenades.

Fifty yards from the patrol he lobbed the grenades and fled. The grass flashed with ear-splitting explosions, panicking the Tiger horses, making them veer, slide and rear. By the time the riders got them under control, Bolan and Ty Ling were past and entering the tree line.

They crashed through another stretch of undergrowth, Ty Ling leading all the time. They came out onto a trail and galloped along it for a mile, then turned off. Here Ty Ling stopped. In the distance they could hear the sound of the pursuing patrol.

The hoofbeats neared, the patrol rode by, and Bolan and Ty Ling exchanged smiles. They resumed their journey, at a walking pace this time. They went cross-country, up a stream, then crossed more savanna and eventually emerged on a logging road.

"I think we're safe now," said Ty Ling.

"You're quite a pathfinder," admitted Bolan.

"I told you I could be useful."

"I need some high ground," he said.

They rode to a ridge and dismounted. Bolan set up the radio and lit a cigarette.

From inside his shirt he brought out a cloth sack and gave it to her. It contained money and jewelry.

At the sight of her jewelry she gasped in surprise.

When she had given him the sack it contained only her money. He had told her not to take anything else, so they would not be encumbered, and she had taken him literally. But after she had gone to the wake it occurred to him that he had been a little harsh, so he added the contents of her jewel box.

"No point in arriving in Germany a refugee," he said.

She held out a diamond bracelet. "For you."

"I don't wear jewelry, but thanks," he replied with a smile.

"For your wife," she said.

"I don't have one."

"You may some day."

"I doubt it," he said. "I believe in it, yeah. I'm told that love over the years makes you live longer. But I'm not made for marriage. Thanks all the same."

Ty Ling handed him the sack. "Please keep it for me." She had no pockets.

They waited for midnight. On these missions it was SOP that when a man failed to answer a radio check, his partner went on a twenty-four-hour standby, turning on the set at midnight for five minutes, three days running.

"What point is there in radioing now if they left this morning?" asked Ty Ling.

"They were *supposed* to leave this morning," said Bolan. "That doesn't mean they actually left. Often extract times are changed at the last moment. The weather interferes or some machinery breaks down. Things seldom work the way they're planned."

A lightning bolt zigzagged on the horizon. A storm was approaching. Already over the next range they could see a mass of dark clouds.

"It is midnight," she said, looking up from her watch.

Bolan turned on the set, gave it a half minute to warm up, then pressed the talk button. "This is Phoenix calling Nark. Over."

The radio hissed silently. Occasionally loud crackling broke in as lightning flashed. But there was no reply.

"This is Phoenix to Nark," Bolan tried again. "Come in, Nark, or Heath or anyone else."

The radio went on hissing and crackling.

"What will we do if they have left after all?" asked Ty Ling.

"I don't know yet," replied Bolan. "We could take a train as you suggested."

"Or we could try leaving by river," said Ty Ling. "It might be safer and quicker. The trains don't run every day. We could go down the Tyak River. I know a village on it. It's not far from here. They might sell us a sampan."

"There's an idea," said Bolan. He tried calling again. No answer.

A bolt of lightning lit the sky, and this time they heard a rumble. The storm was approaching fast.

"We'll have to find shelter," said Ty Ling.

"Are there any villages in the area?" asked Bolan.

"Only the village I mentioned," said Ty Ling. "On the other side of the next range."

"Phoenix to Nark," Bolan went on. To her he said, "We'll have to get you some clothes."

Ty Ling wore a white silk cheongsam. In the Orient, white is the color of mourning. Now it was shredded from their ride. But even in a torn dress she looked like a million dollars, Bolan observed. Not only was Ty Ling a beautiful woman, she had class. She told him her mother, who died when she was a child, was a Chinese princess.

"What time is it?" he asked.

"Five past," said Ty Ling.

Suddenly the radio blared. "Nark to Phoenix. Over."

Bolan started in surprise. "What do you know?" he exclaimed. He pressed the talk button. "This is Phoenix."

"Greetings," said Nark. "Where are you?"

Bolan told him his story. "What about you?"

The extract from Thailand had been canceled due to Thai air activity. The attack on the Tiger hardsite had raised something of a hornets' nest. Stony Man Farm had ordered them to cross the border into Burma where they would be safer.

"You still have the chopper?" asked Bolan.

"Negative," said Nark. "Damage was more complicated than Heath thought. That's why we couldn't come looking for you. What is your present position?"

"The name of the village," Bolan asked Ty Ling.

"Pegu," she replied.

"We're one range south of a village called Pegu," Bolan told Nark.

There was a pause as Nark checked it on the map. "You're only a day's ride from our location," said Nark.

"What time is extract?" asked Bolan.

"Control will advise this morning," said Nark. "They'll be sending helicopters this time. I doubt they'll arrive before nightfall. Correct that—Heath says they could arrive during the day. Seems we have an overflight agreement with Burma. But if you're not here we could pick you up. There's a trail."

"Okay," said Bolan, "we'll bed in Pegu for the night and head for your location in the morning. If the birds arrive before us, you'll come to meet us. Fly along the trail. Agreed?"

"Ten-ten," said Nark.

They arranged for radio checks and signed off.

Bolan dismantled the antenna. "The way things are going you'll be in Düsseldorf by the weekend," he told Ty Ling.

"And you, where will you be?" she asked.

"Home in bed sleeping," he replied. "After this I'm taking a week off just to sleep." He loaded the radio on his back and helped her to her feet. "How long will it take to get to Pegu?" he asked.

"Two or three hours," she replied.

They mounted their horses and rode off. Everything was going perfectly . . . so far.

15

Bolts of lightning illuminated the village. Several hundred houses, some on the ground, others on stilts, lay astride a bend in the river. A wooden bridge linked the two sides. On horseback, dripping with water, Bolan and Ty Ling observed it from a nearby ridge. The storm continued unabated, sheets of rain sweeping the countryside, trees creaking in the wind.

"Who are they?" Bolan shouted above the noise.

"Kachin," Ty Ling shouted back. A tribe of Montagnards.

"Looks all right to me," said Bolan. If there were Tiger soldiers around, he would have seen horses.

"Please, let's go," said Ty Ling, her teeth chattering from the cold.

They descended the slope and rode into the village, sloshing through pools of water, hooves sinking in mud. Bolan reined by the first house that looked big enough to accommodate visitors. He dismounted, went up to Ty Ling, and she slid into his arms. No point in both of them getting their feet muddy.

He kicked the door open on the Montagnard principle of your home is my home and carried her in. Inside was a large room with a beaten earth floor on which glowed a fire. They threw logs on the fire and pulled up stools.

A pair of feet shuffled from behind a partition, and a man in a nightcap appeared. He and Bolan exchanged grunts, then the Montagnard pulled up a stool and joined them. A conversation got underway with Ty Ling translating from Burmese to English.

The gist of it was that they were welcome to stay, and the Montagnard would sell them food for their journey as well as feed for their horses. He also would sell Ty Ling a black pajama suit. Everything would cost five dollars, which Bolan gave him.

Bolan went outside and led the horses to the Montagnard's stable, a roof supported by poles. He unsaddled them, gave them hay and water, and walked back to the house. The storm was finally letting up. On the horizon Bolan could see clear sky. The helicopters could come.

When he got back Ty Ling already wore the black suit. Her dress was suspended from rafters over the fire. On the ground lay two sleeping mats with blankets, and by the fire was a low wicker table with a bottle of tieu and glasses. There was also a plate of dried pig intestines to nibble on, a Montagnard delicacy.

"Take off your suit," said Ty Ling. "You'll catch cold."

Bolan undressed in the shadows. He wrapped himself in a blanket and joined her by the fire. She took his suit and, using a pole, hung it from the rafters.

"What about your socks and underwear?" she asked.

"They're on the mat," he said.

"They have to dry, too," she said. She fetched them and hung them up in turn. She resumed her seat by the fire, poured a glass of tieu, and handed it to Bolan.

He took the glass. "What about you?" he said.

"I don't drink," she replied. She held out the plate of dried food.

Bolan took a handful and munched. It was delicious. He chased it down with the whiskey. "Who's our host?" he asked.

"His name is Alosak," said Ty Ling. "He's got three wives. Each has a house. He rotates a week with each wife." She took a piece of dried food. "What do you think of polygamy?"

Bolan smiled. "Never having been married I don't have an opinion."

"I once had a Montagnard patient who had four wives," said Ty Ling. "This was at the hospital in Mandalay. He said it worked out very well. The wives fought each other and left him in peace." Ty Ling gave Bolan one of her scrutinizing looks. "I'm surprised no woman has hooked you yet."

"I wouldn't be much of a husband," said Bolan. "Always away."

"I don't know," mused Ty Ling, surveying him. She was about to say something, then changed her mind. She refilled his empty glass. "Where will the helicopters take us?"

"Indian Ocean, probably," said Bolan. "We have an island base in the Bay of Bengal. From there we'll take a plane. Most likely it will stop in Frankfurt to refuel. You can fly on from there to Düsseldorf. Only a hundred and twenty miles from Frankfurt."

"I've never been to Germany," said Ty Ling. "Gunther says...." She stopped, seeing Bolan's raised hand.

From outside the door came the sound of feet and hooves sloshing through water and mud. They could also hear the sound of webbing, buckles and metal. It sounded like an army on the march.

The Montagnard appeared from behind the partition. All three listened to the column march by. The sound receded, and Bolan asked the Montagnard to find out who they were. While their host investigated, Bolan dressed.

The Montagnard returned a quarter of an hour later. Ty Ling translated for Bolan. The column was a unit of the Shans. They had stopped for the night in the village on the other side of the river. Some men were wounded.

"I'm going over," said Ty Ling.

"I'll come with you," said Bolan.

"No," said Ty Ling firmly. "Better if they don't see

you. They could take you for an Englishman. The English have advisers helping the Burmese fight the Shans. Get some rest,'' she said, going out with the Montagnard.

Bolan went back to the fire. A bossy woman if ever there was one. But that was typical of Oriental women. Outwardly docile, behind the scenes they could be slave drivers. Gunther was going to have his life cut out from *A* to *Z*, he reflected.

Stretched out on a mat, he was dozing off when the Montagnard returned. But Ty Ling was not with him. Instead, there entered a tall, intelligent-looking individual in a camouflage uniform topped by a *gaung poung*, the traditional Burmese head scarf.

Four soldiers crossed the threshold after him, all four armed with British Sterling submachine guns. Two carried lanterns, two had their weapons in hand, though the muzzles were pointed at the ground.

"Good evening," said the individual in Oxford-accented English. "I am Captain Yeu of the Shan Liberation Army. I understand you're an American.''

"Yes, I am,'' said Bolan.

"Your name?''

"John Phoenix. Colonel.''

"I won't ask what you are doing here,'' the captain began. "I really don't care. I have come to tell you that Dr. Ty Ling will not be leaving with you in the morning. Our doctor has been killed, and we are requisitioning her services for the duration of the campaign.''

"You can't do that,'' said Bolan.

"Really?'' said the captain, amused.

"I promised to take Dr. Ty Ling with me,'' said Bolan.

"Too bad, isn't it?''

"I intend to keep my promise.''

An annoyed expression crossed the captain's face. "Look, Colonel, I'm trying to be nice about this.

You're an American and we have nothing against Americans. If you were English I would simply have you shot. Let's settle our differences in a civilized manner, shall we?'' He held out his hand. ''Your gun belt, please.''

At that, the two muzzles rose.

There are times when discretion is the better part of valor, and Bolan chose this to be one of them. He unbuckled his belt and handed it over. The captain passed it to one of the soldiers and spoke in Shan. Another soldier held up a lantern and inspected the room. The AK-74 and the radio went the way of the gun belt.

''I need my radio to get out of the country,'' said Bolan.

''Or perhaps to tip off the Burmese,'' said the captain. ''You should consider yourself lucky we're letting you go alive, Colonel.''

Bolan smiled easily.

''Your protest is noted,'' the captain acknowledged sarcastically. ''Meanwhile, I advise you not to try any heroics. There will be four men on guard outside. You'll be escorted out of the village at daybreak.'' He opened the door. ''Good night.''

Good night but not goodbye, thought Bolan, watching him leave. *No way am I leaving Burma without Ty Ling. A promise is a promise.*

IN THE MORNING he was awakened by the crowing of cocks. Light filtered through cracks in the mat walls. The household was already up. They served him pancakes and tea, which he took outside to eat. As soon as he stepped through the door, bolts snapped.

''Okay, okay,'' he gestured, calming the four guards. ''Just came out to take some fresh air.''

He squatted down and ate. It was sunrise, and the sun was streaking the sky red and violet. There wasn't a cloud in sight. The helicopters would come for sure.

A couple of soldiers appeared, walking from the river. They came up to the guards and had a conversation in Shan. It was about him, he could tell.

One of the soldiers, a corporal, motioned to him to come. "We go," he said in English.

Bolan downed his tea and returned the mug to the Montagnard. Pancake in hand he walked with them across the bridge. In a field of grazing land, beyond the houses on the other side, the Shan unit was undergoing morning inspection prior to marching out.

There were several hundred soldiers, including two or three hundred riders. The riders were being inspected by Yeu. Bolan caught sight of Ty Ling in the front row, a man's raincoat over her shoulders, a wide straw hat on her head.

Bolan's spirits rose. He would get a chance to talk to her, to tell her not to lose heart, that he would not abandon her, that no matter what, he would rescue her.

But he was deluding himself, for as he approached the riders, Yeu rode to meet him. The corporal stopped the procession, and his sidekick poked the muzzle of his gun in Bolan's back. It was clear they did not want him to go any farther.

"Good morning, Colonel," said Yeu cheerfully.

"Good morning, Captain," Bolan replied. "I wonder if you could ask my escort not to poke me with his gun. It could go off."

Yeu spoke to the man in Shan, and the other lowered the weapon. "Done," said Yeu. "Any other requests?"

"I would like to say goodbye to Dr. Ty Ling."

"That, I regret, is not possible."

"Why not?"

"It is not possible, Colonel," Yeu repeated. "In which direction do you wish to go?"

"I am heading east," said Bolan. "But where is my horse?"

"Your horse has been requisitioned by the Shan

Liberation Army,'' replied Yeu. Again he spoke to the man in Shan. ''Have a nice trip.'' He touched the peak of his cap and rode off.

''We go,'' said the corporal.

But Bolan did not budge. He stood there with his eyes on Ty Ling, trying to decide how he could let her know he would return for her. He did not want to call out. It could antagonize the Shans who might decide she was going to cause trouble and have her beaten later.

The soldier behind him brought the muzzle of his gun up and pushed him with it.

So Bolan simply raised his hand.

In reply, Ty Ling gave him a wave, a sad, resigned wave, the gesture of someone who was not expecting to see him again.

Bolan's throat tightened. She did not expect to see him again, yet she did not ask for her money or jewels.

They set out on the trail in the direction of the rising sun. Walls of steam rose from the jungle. By noon the countryside would be completely dry, Bolan told himself.

So much the better, because with all that rising steam the helicopters could miss him.

Bolan was sure the helicopters would look for him. That was not the problem. The problem was that he still did not know in which direction the Shans were taking Ty Ling. He had hoped to engage the house guards in conversation that morning, but the arrival of the corporal spoiled his plan.

This pair was his last chance. He must not let it go by. He must get into conversation with them before they left him. Unfortunately, the speed at which they moved was not conducive to talking.

The two soldiers kept up a grueling pace, barreling up and down the hills like goats. The Montagnards can do this because they always walk on the balls of their feet to avoid jarring the nerve in the heel.

"Shoot me if you like, but I'm taking a rest," said Bolan. He sat down by a tree. "I'm not used to walking like Montagnards," he lied, wiping sweat from his face with his sleeve.

The soldier said something to the corporal. The other announced, "We take a rest. But not long."

"Agreed," said Bolan. He watched them squat down and light up cigarettes. "That was not nice of the captain to take my horse," he began.

"We need horses to fight," said the corporal.

"In Burma horses expensive," said the soldier. "Not like in America. In America plenty horses. Cowboys. Bang! Bang!"

Both men laughed.

"Have you been fighting long?"

"Me five years," said the corporal.

"Me three," said the soldier.

"A long time," said Bolan.

"Not so long," said the corporal. "Some men fight ten, twenty years. Shans fighting for independence since end of war against Japanese." He meant World War II.

"Where will you fight next?"

"What you mean?" asked the corporal.

"Where is your unit going to fight after the village?"

"We are not allowed to tell you," said the corporal.

"What about yourselves, where will you go when you leave me on the ridge?"

"We join unit."

So. They knew which route the unit was taking, Bolan realized. Now part two of the plan. He stretched himself on his back, hands clasped behind his head, and closed his eyes.

"No sleeping," said the corporal.

"Don't worry," said Bolan. "I won't. I just have a headache."

The soldiers went on smoking in silence. After a while the corporal called, "American."

Bolan ignored him, pretending to be sleeping.

"American, we must go."

Bolan did not budge.

The corporal finished his cigarette and came to Bolan. "Get up," he said, shaking him.

"Let me sleep," Bolan mumbled.

The soldier joined the corporal. Each took an arm and they pulled. "Get up!"

"Okay, okay," Bolan said sleepily.

Bolan's hands closed around their wrists as if to pull himself up. Suddenly he sprang to his feet, pushing and twisting their arms. The soldiers screamed in pain. It was a *yonkio* hold in jujitsu.

"On your knees!" Bolan snarled.

As they went down, he let go of the soldier and delivered a closed-fisted chop to the base of his neck. The soldier went out cold. Bolan disarmed the corporal and ordered him to lie on the ground, facedown.

He took a *dah*, a Burmese machete, and with an eye on the corporal, gun in one hand, he proceeded to chop lianas with the *dah*. He tied them both, then resuscitated the soldier.

They resumed the journey, Bolan walking behind them, holding the Sterling. Once again he was a free man.

"Where are we going?" asked the corporal.

"To the next ridge," said Bolan.

They reached it an hour later. Bolan found a nearby clearing and tied the Shans to trees. He prepared a bonfire with leaves and twigs, packing the inside with wet leaves so it would give off smoke. Then he sat down under a tree, the Sterling in his lap.

"What we wait for?" asked the corporal.

"My helicopters. They will come to pick me up."

"When will they come?"

"This afternoon, maybe. Or maybe tonight. We will wait until they come. And when they come you must tell me where your unit is going so I can get my woman back.''

"We will not tell you," said the corporal. "If we tell you, the captain will kill us."

"And if you don't tell me, I will kill you," said Bolan. "I don't want to, but I will. I am sure you would do the same if someone stole your woman."

"We did not steal your woman," said the soldier.

"Yes, but by not telling me where she is going, you are helping another man steal her. Same thing."

"We are soldiers," he went on. "We must obey orders."

"And I am a man," Bolan retorted. "A man has a duty to defend his woman. Is that not right?"

"We still won't tell you," said the corporal.

"We shall see," said Bolan. "We shall see."

16

A trio of dots in the sky, the helicopters flew toward him. As they neared, Bolan recognized them as a Chinook cargo and two Huey gunships. They flew in pyramid formation, low and slow, following the trail, obviously looking for him.

He ran to the bonfire and lit it. At first there were only flames, but as the fire spread to the wet leaves inside, smoke rose. Immediately one of the gunships flew ahead to investigate. It passed over the clearing and circled.

Bolan took off his shirt and waved it, mainly so they could see the color of his skin, in Asia the surest ID of all. But the crew was not waving back. Something was making them suspicious. The side gunner panned his weapons as if he were shooting it.

The second helicopter joined in, and the sky filled with the clatter of blades. The gunner of the second helicopter pointed out something in the clearing to a man inside.

Suddenly Bolan understood. It was the soldiers under the trees. To the gunners it must have appeared as if they were hiding and that Bolan was the bait for an ambush. Bolan ran to the corporal and brought him out in the open, pointing to his tied wrists.

That did it. The first gunner held out a thumbs-up, the Hueys widened their circle, and the Chinook approached. It had been sitting out the inspection in the sky at a safe distance.

The helicopter came to a hover above Bolan, the

shadow of its huge shape filling the clearing. Treetops swayed from the rotorwash. From portholes gunners leaned out inspecting the ground.

Bolan waited for the message container that would tell him where to proceed for the pickup. The clearing was too small for the Chinook to land. Instead, Nark stepped out the side door and sailed down harnessed to a rope. The Chinook was equipped with a winch.

"I have passengers," Bolan shouted over the din. He held up two fingers.

"There's room," Nark shouted back.

Nark took off his harness, then they cut the corporal's bonds and harnessed him in. Nark waved to the crew chief in the doorway, and the corporal sailed up like a package. The soldier was next, then Bolan, and then finally Nark. The helicopter moved off.

"Where's your lady friend?" asked Nark, taking a seat next to Bolan on the side canvas bench.

Bolan told him what had happened and what he proposed to do. "Who's the flight chief?" Bolan asked.

"Our pilot," said Nark, "Captain Opersdorf." Nark spoke into Bolan's ear. The din in the helicopter was overwhelming. "But I wouldn't say anything about promises. I don't think he'd understand. Better keep it pro. Say she's an agent. We blew up the hardsite, by the way."

Bolan gripped his arm and nodded his thanks. He went to see Opersdorf.

The flight commander listened to Bolan's request with a decided lack of enthusiasm. Tonight was bridge night on the U.S.S. *Idaho* at anchor off Kobe Island. Anything that would interfere with his presence at the table was most unwelcome.

"Colonel, this is highly irregular," Opersdorf replied. "Our orders are to fly you directly to Kobe. Nothing in them says anything about additional extracts in route."

"I realize that, Captain, but it's imperative the agent be rescued."

"No, Colonel, I can't order my men into a shoot-out without proper authority. For that I need a written order and it has to be through channels."

"There will be no need for a shoot-out," Bolan replied. "A show of force will do. And there's no time to go through channels. I'm asking a favor of you, Captain."

"Sorry, Colonel, but a combat mission is too much of a favor. What if one of the helos is downed? How will I explain that? I was doing you a favor?"

"Okay, Captain," said Bolan. "I'll go after the agent myself. Give me a minute to check, and I'll tell you where you can let me off."

Bolan left and returned by Nark's side.

"Well?" said Nark.

"No dice," said Bolan. He explained what he intended to do.

"You can't go after her alone," Nark protested. "You'll get killed."

"She saved my life, Nark," Bolan replied. "A good enough reason for me to risk mine." He glanced at the Shans.

The soldiers were huddled on the bench with the expression of Earthmen captured by Martians. Neither had been in a helicopter before. In their brown flight suits and helmets with huge black visors, the crew did indeed resemble spacemen.

"The crew chief says he can squeeze the information out of them," said Nark.

"I'll do my own dirty work," said Bolan, rising.

But he still needed the crew chief's help, so he went to talk to him. The other handed him a belt with a safety strap.

Bolan moved to the Shans and leaned over the corporal.

"The time has come for you to give me the information," he said.

He led the corporal to the rear of the machine. "Stand here."

Bolan put on the belt and attached the safety strap to the railing overhead. That way if there was a struggle he would not fall out with the corporal. "Where are they taking my woman?" he asked.

"I cannot tell you," replied the corporal.

Bolan nodded to the crew chief. The other pressed a lever, machinery hummed, and the rear ramp opened revealing the void below. The corporal's Adam's apple did a jig, and his eyes widened in terror.

"If you don't tell me," said Bolan, "I will push you out. When your body hits the ground it will be like hamburger. A hyena will eat it in no time. Your spirit will be imprisoned in the hyena. And what for? You think your friend won't talk when he sees what happened to you?"

The corporal looked at his comrade, but the other was not even looking. In that instant the corporal knew the soldier would talk. That was why he was looking away, so as not to reveal the truth in his eyes. The corporal looked at the void below, then back to his partner, then to the others.

The eyes of the long noses surveyed him with indifference. It was as if he were already dead. A yard away was death. Death! And for what? It occurred to him that he could always invent some story for Captain Yeu. Or he could quit the army. All kinds of possibilities lay open. . . as long as he lived.

"They took the Kohimo trail," he blurted out.

"What is their final destination?" asked Bolan.

"The town of Bur."

Bolan went to Nark who opened a map.

"What time did they leave?" asked Nark.

"About seven," said Bolan.

Nark glanced at his watch. "They should be entering the Plain of Chuk."

"About that," said Bolan. "I'll ask him to drop me on the other side."

He went to see Opersdorf. "I'd like to be dropped off on the northern edge of the Plain of Chuk. Is that possible?"

The pilot considered the request in silence. "What will you do after we drop you off?" he asked finally.

"Wait, then follow them until they camp for the night," said Bolan. "I'll attempt a rescue during the night."

"Alone?"

"Alone."

Opersdorf considered this. "Taking you there will entail a half-hour detour," he said.

"If that's too long, you can drop me off right now," said Bolan.

"I didn't mean that," said Opersdorf. "I meant if we're going to make a detour we might as well go whole hog and make the attempt with you."

Bolan smiled.

"This is Lema one to Lema two and three," Opersdorf drawled into his radio. "We're changing course." He gave the gunships the new headings. The flight turned north.

"How do you propose we go about this?" Opersdorf asked Bolan.

"We land ahead of the column and I talk to them."

"What if they take you hostage?" said Opersdorf. "Then where will we be? I'd rather you negotiated from the air. We have a bullhorn on board."

Opersdorf called the crew chief and told him to get the bullhorn out. Next he briefed the gunships and his own machine gunners. They flew on.

"The Shan soldiers in the back," said Opersdorf. "What do we do with them?"

"Drop them off near some village," said Bolan. "But after the rescue."

The plain appeared, a vast stretch of grassland dotted with an occasional tree. Opersdorf gave Bolan a pair of field glasses. As Bolan brought them to his eyes, his heart sank. He and Nark had miscalculated the column's speed. It was traveling much faster than they had figured. Instead of being on this side of the plain, it was nearing the other.

"Going to be touch and go," said Opersdorf, observing the plain.

The plain would have been a perfect place to attempt a rescue had they arrived an hour or two earlier. They would have had time to reconnoiter the force and identify Ty Ling—and time in which to do some selective shooting in case the column did not comply with their demands.

At the approach of the helicopters, the foot soldiers scattered, throwing themselves into the grass while the horsemen broke into a gallop, heading for the safety of the tree line ahead. The tree line was only about three miles away. Too little time for a rescue.

"We're out of luck, Colonel," said Opersdorf.

"An eagle snatch, Captain," Bolan said. "Let me try it!"

"Move fast, Colonel."

A minute later Bolan emerged from the side of the Chinook wearing a harness. He sailed down at the end of a rope, coming to a halt ten feet above the heads of the galloping horsemen. He spotted Ty Ling right away. She was near the front, her horse attached by a long rope to the saddle of a horseman ahead of her.

"Agent is at eleven o'clock," said Bolan into the side mike of his helmet. "The wide straw hat. A hundred yards from me."

"We see her," said Opersdorf. He was leaning out of

a porthole coordinating the operation while the copilot flew the helicopter.

"Drop me five feet, left ten yards," said Bolan.

Slowly Bolan flew over the heads of the galloping riders. On either side flew the gunships, their side gunners pointing their weapons down at the riders.

"Right two yards."

Now he could hear the thunder of the hooves, could smell the horses' sweat. Behind him he heard a shout of surprise. A burst of fire rent the sky as a Huey fired at a rider about to take a potshot at him.

"Slow down a little!"

Only two riders were left between him and Ty Ling. A tree passed him. The second Huey fired. Another tree passed him. Now he was directly behind Ty Ling, her back approaching him. Coming. Coming.

"Down two feet for pickup."

Two yards, a yard. He bumped against the horse's rump, a hoof kicked him in the leg, he bent his knees, the movement swung him out, he bumped the side of the rump.

Ty Ling turned. A frightened cry escaped her lips. Then she recognized him through his goggles.

"Let go of the stirrups!" he shouted.

The rope swayed. He came away, then swayed back to the horse. This time he threw his arms around her. The animal sidestepped, and she fell out of the saddle. But he had her.

"I got her, I got her," he shouted into the mike. "Take me up!"

The galloping horsemen receded as he rose holding on to Ty Ling with all his might, fighting the sway, fighting gravity, his mind empty of all thought but one, to hold on!

The din from the Chinook overhead grew, he felt the air blast of its blade, heard his clothes flapping, and then he was bumping against its side. Hands reached out and pulled them in. He had done it!

The crew chief helped Ty Ling to a side bench while Bolan took off his helmet, harness, and goggles. Opersdorf came up to him and shook his hand. The gunners shook his hands, everyone shook his hand.

A feat like his stirred the imagination, warmed the heart: a twentieth-century knight swooping out of the sky to save a lady in distress. Chivalry was not dead.

As for the lady, she stared at him with such emotion in her eyes that he lowered his. As he sat down beside her, Ty Ling gripped his hand with almost animal ferocity in a secret message he preferred not to decode.

And that's how they flew out of Burma, and that's how the mission ended, with the Executioner and his victim's daughter holding hands.

"ACHTUNG! ACHTUNG!"

The loudspeakers at the Frankfurt airport announced the final call for Lufthansa Flight 167 for Düsseldorf. Bolan touched Ty Ling's arm and pointed upward. She hung up the pay phone, and they set out for the boarding gate.

"Gunther is meeting me at the airport," she said. "We will marry next month. Will you come to the wedding?"

"I'll try."

"I would like you to give me away. Would you?"

Bolan's throat tightened. "Yes, it would be an honor to give you away," he said. "I'll come for certain."

They arrived at the gate. Ty Ling got her boarding pass ready and turned to Bolan, eyes glistening.

Her arms went around his neck, and she pressed her mouth to his. Then, without a word, she was gone.

Bolan walked back to the bar to rejoin Hal Brognola. The U.S. president's special assistant, who had been attending a conference in Berlin, had flown in to meet him.

"The lady left?" he asked as Bolan resumed his seat.

"Yes, she's gone."

"Some woman."

"Yeah," said Bolan. He toyed with a matchbook.

Brognola reached under the table for his briefcase. "Received a report on Galloping Horse this morning," he said. "We're picking them up like flies. We've won the battle, Mack."

"*A* battle, Hal, *a* battle," said Bolan pensively. "In the fight against evil there is no final victory. For that you would have to destroy the whole human race because evil lurks in all of us. New Tigers will rise from the ashes of the old."

"I guess you're right," Brognola sighed. "A disturbing thought."

"Not really," Bolan reflected aloud. "In the process of fighting evil, a person also discovers good. That, too, is in all of us. And that's what makes the fight worthwhile."

EPILOGUE

Mack Bolan is a soldier, and he fights a soldier's battle. His munitions are all real articles used by combatmen everywhere, and whatever Bolan accomplishes with his weaponry is within the realm of human achievement.

But he also fights a more cosmic war, in which good and evil are far greater concepts than mere weapons in the arsenal of stale ideas. To Bolan, Armageddon is not some future mythical war to be waged between God and Satan—it is here, now, and always has been, as the life force of this planet continually strives to perfect itself.

To achieve every possibility of human excellence within his reach, Bolan must keep moving.

The entire world is on his ass. He must keep moving.

To stay alive.

For the horrors have only just begun. . . .

DON PENDLETON ON
MACK BOLAN

The heroin trade is Mack Bolan's enemy in *Tiger War*, as Mack fights in the jungles of Thailand to free the youth of the United States from the plague of drug addiction. To my mind, damnation is never too soon for those who defend Tiger Enterprises, Asia Minor's seamy equivalent of the Mafia.

Tom Jagninski is a tried and true war writer, and he furthers the fate of The Executioner with explosive images born of real combat. Jagninski, a former war correspondent in Asia and Africa, knows from his experience with the 1st Recon Battalion, USMC, how to cull vivid details of jungle survival from jungle warfare—such as the fireflies carried by the Montagnards in cages on their backs. Jagninski's sure-handed professionalism cannot help but light the old fire in Mack's belly.

I have felt for many years that we live in a savage world. I'm not talking about the primitive kind of savages. I'm saying there are savages sitting on the boards of some of the world's most prodigious organizations. Savagery is a state of mind that crops up *everywhere*.

Mack Bolan will never tolerate a world where Savage Man survives. He proves this to a heroic and tragic extent in The Executioner #62, *Day of Mourning*. It's the first book in a trilogy of bereavement, betrayal and newly forged mission that will curl your hair with its realism. Be prepared for a shocker!

Don Pendleton

HE'S EXPLOSIVE.
HE'S UNSTOPPABLE.
HE'S MACK BOLAN!

e learned his deadly skills in Vietnam…then put them to use by destroying e Mafia in a blazing one-man war. Now **Mack Bolan** is back to battle new reats to freedom, the enemies of justice and democracy—and he's recruited me high-powered combat teams to help. **Able Team**—Bolan's famous Death quad, now reborn to tackle urban savagery too vicious for regular law forcement. And **Phoenix Force**—five extraordinary warriors handpicked Bolan to fight the dirtiest of anti-terrorist wars around the world.

Fight alongside these three courageous forces for freedom in all-new, lse-pounding action-adventure novels! Travel to the jungles of South America, e scorching sands of the Sahara and the desolate mountains of Turkey. d feel the pressure and excitement building page after page, with nonstop tion that keeps you enthralled until the explosive conclusion! Yes, Mack Bolan d his combat teams are living large…and they'll fight against all odds to otect our way of life!

w you can have all the new Executioner novels delivered right to ur home!

u won't want to miss a single one of these exciting new action-adventures. d you don't have to! Just fill out and mail the coupon following and we'll enter ur name in the Executioner home subscription plan. You'll then receive r brand-new action-packed books in the Executioner series every other nth, delivered right to your home! You'll get two **Mack Bolan** novels, one **le Team** and one **Phoenix Force**. No need to worry about sellouts at bookstore…you'll receive the latest books by mail as soon as they come off presses. That's four enthralling action novels every other month, featuring all ee of the exciting series included in The Executioner library. Mail the card ay to start your adventure.

EE! Mack Bolan bumper sticker.

en we receive your card we'll send your four explosive Executioner vels and, absolutely FREE, a Mack Bolan "Live Large" bumper sticker! This ge, colorful bumper sticker will look great on your car, your bulletin board, or ywhere else you want people to know that you like to "Live Large." And you are der no obligation to buy anything—because your first four books come on a day free trial! If you're not thrilled with these four exciting books, just return m to us and you'll owe nothing. The bumper sticker is yours to keep, FREE!

Don't miss a single one of these thrilling novels…mail the card now, while 're thinking about it. And get the Mack Bolan bumper sticker FREE!

BOLAN FIGHTS AGAINST ALL ODDS TO DEFEND FREEDOM

Mail this coupon today!

Continued high praise for Mack Bolan's new war!

"Well written, well researched, fast-paced and has a huge following!"

—*The Voice: Book Talk by Gary Roen*

"The Executioner is a bestseller—the leading male fiction in the country—because Bolan has principles about what he thinks is right and he's not afraid to defend those principles."

—*The Virginia-Pilot*

"I do like this series . . . I read each battle in the new war as the book is released. The key to my attachment is that they are fast paced, fun and enjoyable. The Executioner is one of the *good* paperback series!"

—*Echoes: Book Reviews by Link Hullas*

"Power packed! Right out of tomorrow's headlines."

—*Stag*

GOLD EAGLE